BRIAN'S LAW

AND OTHER
SHORT STORIES

Brian's Law

And Other Short Stories

by

Bernard Scott

LOGOS INSTITUTE PRESS
2013

The short story, "Night of Holy Innocence," first appeared in the 2010 Christmas Edition of the Catholic weekly *The Wanderer*. It is reprinted here with permission. "True and False," appeared among the prizewinners in Tuscany Press's 2012 collection of short stories and is reprinted here with permission. "The Edge of the Coffin" was a finalist in the Tuscany Press collection of prize-winning short stories for 2013.

Other Works by the Author

Secret of Lost Mountain
Adventure/Mystery Novel
(Finalist in Tuscany Press 2012 Best Novel Award)
ISBN 978-0-9801174-7-9

The Heart Hath Its Reasons
Novella
ISBN 978-0-9801174-9-3

The Mystery of Work
Anthology
ISBN 978-0-9801174-1-7

*The Redeemer's Call to
Consecrated Souls*
Translation from the French
ISBN 978-0-9801174-6-2

LOGOS INSTITUTE PRESS
Tarpon Springs, FL

TABLE OF CONTENTS

I Heard Their Laughter

I MEANT THEM NO HARM but they were bothering me. Try to understand. Until they came I had lived alone on the top floor of this abandoned building for all of thirteen years and eight months, isolated by deliberate intent in this forsaken, cold-water flat right beneath the roof, disturbing no one, desiring nothing more than to pursue these final days in unmolested solitude. In all those years I have had no neighbors to assail me with their have-a-nice-day vapidities. Except for infrequent trips out for food and to cash my miserly pension check, I avoid going down to the streets below. I wish to impress upon you that I seek no company, I need no one. Socially speaking I am as *absent* a person as you can be and still remain in the world. And I am content that it be that way. Even my name on the mailbox in the lobby of this wretched building is no longer legible. Perhaps I should darken the letters now that—I dread to say it —this building, accommodatingly empty for so long, is taking on tenants. Perhaps I shall redraw my name, right at the end, as my epitaph, so that these intruders will understand that this weird, unnamed presence up here on the top floor had been a real person, he too had a name. But then I ask you, why should I?

I trust I have made myself clear. Until now I bothered no one and gave no one cause to bother me. I wish to impress this upon you strongly in view of these measures I felt obliged to take. I have no history of arrests, of formal complaints against me. I have always sought to keep myself invisible to the police. If these intruders on my floor complain about me, what do I care? What do they mean to me? Nothing, I can assure you of that. The entire world could expire at my feet and it would mean nothing to me, *nada*, just as my demise will mean *zero* to it. And I am reconciled to this. I have long since given up the notion of meaning anything to anyone, even to myself. I know in my bones I can never add a sum like the one I subtracted years ago. I have long since even ceased to try.

I hope you will understand why this new circumstance has become so calamitous. Why I had to do these unpleasant things. Let me explain. Thirteen years ago I was homeless, passing sleepless nights in the city's subways, and my days wandering aimlessly down its streets, like a Hamlet pondering reasons to stay or not stay in this world. And finding none, I might add, yet not knowing what to do, where to go, how to abide a life that could never come to anything, and worse, not knowing even how to end it. Then, by happy circumstance, I chanced upon this building with its huge CONDEMNED sign, this vacant little apartment structure squeezed between dark, windowless warehouses. It happened that the entrance door was ajar, almost as if somehow I had been expected. I immediately went in. The interior was unlit with the dead quiet of a mausoleum, all perfectly suited to the state I was in. I saw at once that if I were to hole away in a building like this, I could take my time for what, logically speaking, lay ahead. So I began to explore the premise. The elevator of course wasn't working so I climbed the stairs and peeked in on each floor. The halls were short with just a few flats. Tall, dirty, hall windows at both ends let in light enough for me to try the doors. Invariably they were locked tight.

On the third floor I received a shock. As I emerged from the stairwell, I practically ran down an old, decrepit, white-haired woman coming toward me. The old lady jerked back like she'd seen a ghost but I danced around as if I was absolutely delighted to meet her (which I was actually). I finally got her to talking. She told me she had been born in this building, as had her mother before her. For the last five years she was the only tenant left, the last to go. The old woman would have gone on with her stories, but I broke in and asked if any of the flats might be unlocked. She understood my intent well enough and pointed above her head. "The top floor," she said, "under the roof." I kissed her hand (I did) and went up there at once.

Like the others, the hall on the top floor had three flats. The two at the ends were locked tight, but when I turned the handle of the door to the middle flat, it opened, bless her, just as she said. Heavy, stale air

3

almost chocked me as I stepped in. The flat, being in the middle, was windowless but light from the hall was enough to reveal a small kitchen and a second, interior room. I could see trash strewn all about the linoleum floor. The kitchen was grimy and bare except for a small, dead, gas-burning stove, and happily, a single kitchen chair and table. The table had a newspaper spread out on it, there since the last occupant forsook the place. On it sat an oversized mug, black with dried out coffee, and in the sink a few foul-looking dishes. But what caught my eye was the bed in the second room. Of all good things, a bed! After nights on bone-hard subway seats, an unexpected gift. No matter the mattress sank practically half way to the floor when I spread myself out on it. It all seemed too good to be true—a place hidden away on the top floor of an empty building, utterly cut off from the rest of the world. I knew immediately I had found the perfect venu for my purpose.

Condemned building or not, I preferred to legitimize my residence here if such a thing were possible, so I went down at once to that old lady on the third floor for the landlord's address. And I right away sent him a rent check to see what he would do. What he did was cash it. And I have been sending him a check every month ever since, for 166 months. The whole arrangement was illegal, I'm sure, on both our parts, but no one seemed to care. Certainly not the gas and electric utilities, who turned on service the day they too got their money. That was the one thing necessary. Flats in buildings like this are unheated in winter and uncooled in summer. Winters you use the gas stove in the kitchen, all four burners blazing away if you don't wish to freeze to death. Summers are different. Summers you curse your lot.

I have no complaint against the landlord, a skinflint for sure. I even do not complain about the unearthly rent increase imposed on me last month. (I at least will not have to pay it for long.) But shortly after I received that notice, some agent of his tried to enter my place. I refused to answer his banging. *We have to make an inspection,* he shouted trying to push the door open against my foot. I yelled back through the door there was no need for inspection and he should not waste his time, or mine. After a while I heard him walk away. But that was the harbinger.

One morning soon afterwards, the quiet peace of my floor here under the roof, so suitable to me, was shattered as noisy workmen arrived, opened up the adjoining flats and started tearing out linoleum flooring, slapping paint on the walls and laying down cheap, thin carpets. In each they put in a half-size refrigerator and a tiny kitchen gas stove. And you can be sure, no other source of heat.

It has occurred to me, of course, that we most likely have a new landlord, which explains why the faded "CONDEMNED" sign is gone from the building, why the rent increase, why the elevator is suddenly working, and why, I shudder to think of it, tenants are moving in on the floors below.

And then, three weeks ago, this nightmare arrived on my floor. It was late one morning. I had come up the stairs with my little bag of food (canned beans and water is the sum of what I consume anymore). I

5

noticed at once that the door to the flat on my right was wide open. As I hurried past, a girl stuck her face out, and then out of the corner of my eye a young fellow, and as I got to my door I heard them laugh, a galling laugh I tell you. They were barely adult, which I suppose you could argue might excuse them. But the girl's laughter was especially vexing to me, like a child's.

I hear them through the thin walls all the time now, laughing, even when they're making love. They talk in merry shouts as if what they have to say is always worth a laugh. And I am well aware they laugh at the queer duck next door, the weird one who never takes the elevator. Why should I? For thirteen years I have been content with the stairs and I see no reason to change my habit. Especially now in these final days. But with people moving into the building, a miscalculation was bound to occur.

As it did one week ago. Because of increasing weakness in my legs, I figured it was worth the risk and I pressed the elevator button on my floor. I need-ed to go down for my gas bill which I like to pay on time. But just as the elevator arrived, these two came bursting out of their flat.

"Oh, good!" the girl cried out with her galling laugh, "We're just in time!" (How I despise this voice.) And to be sure her partner joined right in. (I have no idea if he's her husband. Most likely not.)

The elevator doors parted just as they came near and I had little choice but to enter with these two behind me. There we were, the three of us crammed together in this tiny cage of a lift that takes forever.

What does one do in such circumstances? Like any decent soul I kept my eyes on the floor treating them as if they weren't there, expecting from them the same courtesy. But I could feel their shameless gaze creep all over me. When we got to the ground floor, I exited fast as my legs would let me. At the mailbox, out of the edge of my eye, I saw the girl double up with laughter. It was then I truly came to hate them both.

And now, just yesterday, some new intruder has moved into the other flat on my left. Judging from the light footstep in the hall, it must be someone young, a lithe woman perhaps. It's rather strange. I hear nothing through the wall except the sound of water running now and then. Otherwise complete and total absence of sound. If I have to, I can abide a silent, lifeless soul like this. For all I know we may be two of a kind.

The ones to my right are the two to be dealt with. I trust you will understand I could not allow their carrying on day and night this way. As I have said, I need peace and quiet now more than ever, in the little time I have left.

In the time I have left. Why do I tell you that? Why explain myself? Why do I care to tell you anything, who I am, who I was, who I might have been. Why I came here thirteen years and eight months ago, 4983 days to be exact, 17 days short of my allotted 5000 (I keep tally, you see). Why I had to try and chase off these heartless clowns that invaded my private world. And who is this *you* I keep explaining myself to? I have no answer. There is no longer any *you* in my life, not a single soul. Yet, I still have these mocking voices, voices that laugh and say: *Just because you died, it doesn't mean you lived.* You see, before I depart I need someone, somewhere to know I had a life once. I did. And a name, John Mathias. The memory of it eats at me like acid.

I was a mathematician, an established person who enjoyed all the trappings of real existence. I was a tenured, one-man mathematics phenomenon at a first-rate girls' academy (which out of decency I refrain from naming). In reality, I should have been tenured at a top university. I had more than enough talent for that, but as you might know, talent and politics don't sit well together.

Mathias the Math Freak the girls used to call me, behind my back of course. I cannot blame them. Not many took to mathematics, and I did not make it easy for them. I admit that. I used to open my fall semesters with a quotation from the mathematicians' mathematician, Lord Russell: *A mathematician does not need to know what he is talking about, about whether what he is says is true.* Of course my love of irony here would set these rich men's daughters off. One of the bolder ones would always object, *So then why should we listen to you?* I would laugh, actually enjoying her impudence, and announce, *You will listen because of the consequences if you don't.* I would stride up and down and wave my arms, driving the paradox home like the eccentric they took me for, *You will learn that mathematics is a science of necessary consequences. It shares that property with physics. But in mathematics, the consequences, while they have to be necessary, they do not have to be true.* And I would tell them that in this respect mathematics stands alone, despite her many suitors, like a virgin queen, quite content with herself.

By now frowns would darken every young face in the class. *What's mathematics about?* one would mumble. And I would answer gleefully, *It's about nothing! Mathematics is about nothing at all. Or to put it another way, it's only about itself.* By this time someone would shout, *What's it good for then?* And I would tell her, *You cannot ask that question in this class. If you want to know what mathematics is good for, go ask the physics instructor or some engineer. As far as this class is concerned, mathematics is its own reason for being.* I had my fun but, not surprisingly, by the second session half the seats would be empty. The administration wasn't happy about that, but as far as I was concerned, it left me with fewer papers to check, fewer grades to record. You see, I for one felt above consequences, and it would have remained that way except for this other matter. And even that would have worked out if I'd been a good fellow and done the expected thing, the very thing I could not bring myself to do. A day does not go by, barely an hour of the day that I do not reflect on this fact, that had I chosen differently I would not be here beneath the roof of this unheated, god-forsaken building, counting the days.

You realize these are the lamentations of Mathias the Math Freak, half remorseful, half defiant, a man about to depart knowing he never pulled off the one thing expected of a man, to have a life, to add up to something. To put it as bluntly and as frankly as I can, I am a man who for 4983 days has been hiding out from the world, waking up each of those mornings with no good reason to get out of bed, to change the clothes I slept in, to heat up a can of food, spending the time wondering whether today was a good day to go down to the street, whether different air would do me some good, and always ending up just shuffling between rooms, pondering mathematical imponderables. Why, you ask? I don't know how to answer for certain, but generally I conjecture it's because I am cursed, living (or should I say never quite managing to live) under some kind of acid justice, eaten away with memories of a path not taken, of a life, of a Mathias that could have been, but would not agree to be that person.

Her name was Carrie and she was young to be the new English instructor. The real difficulty for me lay in the fact that she was too good, too pure. She had been married, very briefly, an unfortunate marriage that through no fault of hers failed almost immediately. And she had a child by it, a little girl named Celi, who I must say I never got along with. Too much of her father in her. But I got to know and like the mother right away, she was so easy, so unexpectedly good to be with. They happened to assign her the office next to mine, and Carrie hadn't settled in ten minutes before she stuck her sweet lovely face into my doorway. How well I recall the moment. We joked that we knew absolutely nothing about each other's specialties but somehow we hit it off, the spread in age notwithstanding. I felt an unfamiliar stirring when I heard her next door with the students. They were always breaking out into these silly giggles over something I could not grasp. But the sweet sound of her laughter always got to me; I'd look up from my work and have to sort of half-laugh myself.

Before long we began to look for each other between classes and have coffee, and then we started going to movies and school events together. It was all new for me, and frankly a bit scary. I'd lived alone all my life, you see, never had much time for women, never got close to any of them. But Carrie was not any woman. She was different. Almost from the start I found I wanted to be in her company and I'd look for excuses. She seemed to feel that way too, and when I wasn't finding reasons to be in her office, she'd find some need to be in mine. Soon we were dating more seriously, and finally we got into what people call *heavy dating*. It was all new, and very exciting for this inveterate loner.

But there was the matter of this child, Celi. I knew this kid didn't like me, understandable I suppose since it had to seem I was taking her mother from her. But it became a problem. One day Carrie brought her daughter to my office and asked if I would look after her while she took her class. I imagine she was hoping Celi and I would begin to hit it off. I tried my best to entertain the kid, even getting down on the floor with her. *Celi, do you know how to count?* I said. She just looked at me but when I started slowly, *one, two,* she responded *four, three, five.* She was plenty bright and it didn't take much to straighten her out, though I had to use my own fingers as she wouldn't give me hers. Then I did a stupid thing, maximally stupid, something only Mathias the Math Freak would think of. I tried to teach her what *zero* was. As you undoubtedly know, the term means *empty* or *nothing* (*shunya* in Sanskrit, *sifr* in Arabic). And it wasn't until the 12th century that the western world added *zero* to its number system, so to think this little kid could grasp the notion of *sheer emptiness* was idiocy. Like an idiot, though, I tried. I held up my hand with fingers spread wide and then, closing each finger, I counted backwards until all the fingers were gone, *five, four, three, two, one*, and then I rotated my fist in a tight circle and said *zero, Celi, zero*. Then I did the count in the normal order, starting with the closed *zero* fist. She didn't get the point but I kept at it, and she began to cry, really cry. As luck would have it, Carrie came in just then too. It must have looked like I was shaking my fist at the kid. She laughed when I explained later. But then that ironic streak in me really did it. A week after, when I was taking care of the kid again, I said, *Celi, do you remember how to count?* She rattled the numbers off fine, *one, two, three, four, five* (no *zero* of course). But, and may I be forgiven for this, I said, *No Celi, one, two, four, three, five.* I was teasing of course, but the kid became hysterical. Her screaming brought half the floor into my office. The child calmed down by the time Carrie get back, thankfully. I explained what happened and again we laughed. But that's when she told me I would learn to be a father because, and then she dropped the bombshell, she was expecting.

I have to tell you right off that is where the existential fork took place. The last thing in the world I wanted for myself was to multiply and become a father. I did my best to react the way she'd expect but she's smart and she read my mind. I still see her lovely face turn ashen white. She thrust beads into my hand and asked me to pray. Later she begged me to say a rosary with her, but I knew what was going through my mind wasn't prayer. She always had these beads, kissing the little crucifix when we took a meal, even in the school cafeteria. I used to think it touching. This girl was too good to be real.

In her mind, of course, being pregnant had to mean marriage. That was just the way things worked. And anything short of marriage would have been ruinous to us both at this school. There's no chance they would keep an unmarried, pregnant, untenured English instructor, and who knows what they'd do to me once they found out I was the one. My thought was to terminate the pregnancy, the way it is usually done. But I knew there was fat chance of that, not with her, not in a hundred million years. She used to say she wanted scads of kids and when I'd make a face, she'd laugh and say, *Come on, you'll make a good father once you got used to it, once our baby is born.* Until the end it never occurred to Carrie that marriage was not going to happen. I might have considered it actually, if it had been just her, but there was Celi, and there'd be other kids and arguments about more kids. And this religion she was so caught up in: rosaries, crucifixes and all that talk about Christ's blood. I'd had nothing to do with any of it since the funeral Mass for my father, when I was seven. I remember at the wake asking my mother when you die do you transition to infinity or to nullity, and she just

13

smirked at me. Maybe it was the ten dollar words I used. But I never got an answer, nor much of anything else from her after my father died. Perhaps it was anger that made her that way, but from that early age on I decided I couldn't trust her or anyone else, not in this world (and I saw no reason to believe in any other).

But Carrie was not just anyone to me. She was incredibly special and despite these differences, despite even the pregnancy, I was still terribly drawn to her. You have to believe me when I say the impasse worked its agonies on us both. The last time we talked, our eyes were wet in both of us. She said she'd never stop praying this would work out. But what I did the very next day was the only rational course open to me, the only real choice I had in view of the binary circumstance I was in, an act as logical for me as I suppose it was unforgiveable for everyone else. What I did was I left her, without a word, and my position at school as well. I just hopped a bus out of town, leaving behind everything I owned, worked for, and the girl I tried to love. And in truth I did love her in my way, but you see I didn't love her enough. That was the problem. I couldn't abandon myself to her, to love her enough to change who I was and be what she hoped for, the man she told me she used to dream about, the man I decided wasn't going to be me.

I don't know what became of her, or of the pregnancy, nor have I tried to find out. As for the school, I got a lawyer years ago to wrest a measly pension from them, but you can believe my name is never mentioned in those halls. I won't bore you with the details but after that fateful bus ride things never went well. Without a recommendation, no other school would open its doors. I was left alone with myself. I trust what ultimately became of that self will be clear soon enough, to anyone inclined to read these lines, should such a soul even exist. Yes, perhaps an offspring somewhere who wonders about the father she (or he) might have had. May she never doubt I haven't paid for that denial.

*   *   *

Hi. My name is Andy and I am the "husband" who moved in next to the queer old gent that's responsible for the lines above and the incredible words you'll find below. We found these scribblings on the floors of his flat, that's when my wife and I made a deal with the landlord to clean out his place in exchange for a month's rent. Most were torn up and I've had to puzzle them together. I've also added some things I found out about him. I'm an engineer in the making, not a writer, so you'll have to excuse me for my prose.

Anyway, it seemed fitting to record this, given the bloody event involving this guy and the lady tenant on our floor. This woman had taken the flat at the other end of the hall a week or so before this nightmare happening. The new tenant looked like she could have been a model, and what someone like her was doing on the top floor of this dump is a permanent mystery. We'll never know the who and the why of it all, but the poor lady came within inches of losing her life. For all we know maybe in the end she didn't make it either. But my wife and I sure hope she did.

First, I have to defend myself. We never laughed at this character, though God knows there was enough to laugh at. We laughed at our own double-take when we saw him the first time. He wobbled past our door like a strip of bent wire. So thin and stooped over you wondered how he could defy the center of gravity like that and not be on his face.

We know now why he did those weird things to us, why he didn't want us here, why he was trying to scare us away. At the time it struck us as just stupid. Empty bean cans in front of our door, greeting us every morning when we went off to classes. We knew it was him of course. My wife wanted to put the cans right back at his door, with banana peels or apple cores in them. Tit for tat, our garbage for his. But we didn't. We had more positive things to think about, like an unexpected pregnancy. And how a couple of dirt-poor engineering students are to juggle classes and this little one we're soon going to be caring for.

These queer antics of his went on for days — one empty can of beans before our door practically every morning, like clockwork. But then things took a nasty turn. We went out one morning and found a dead rat at our door. That was scary but even so we tried to make light of it. I put it in front of his with a note that this little fellow got lost and asked to be returned where he belongs. What happened next was of another order. The rat was back the next morning, this time with a kitchen knife in it stuck through our note. We didn't waste time getting down to the neighborhood police station. They knew about him and they said they'd take care of it. A burly cop came that afternoon and banged on his door. Eventually he got the old guy to open. We couldn't make out their conversation, only the cop's *loud voice. And he didn't mince his words. After a while the cop came to our door and said he didn't think we'd have any more trouble. He said we maybe should keep our voices down some, and the TV, seeing how sound carries through the walls. We didn't tell him we don't have TV.*

Before I tell you about the tragedy, I should share what I've since learned about our neighbor, to give this sad event some perspective. From his effects we found out that his name is John Mathias. And as you know from what he wrote above, he had been a mathematician. A pretty serious one too. There were notebooks full of equations and what-not all over his flat. Most of the math was way beyond me, but it looked serious whatever it was. On a lark I asked my math professor at City College if he'd ever heard of John Mathias. Believe it or not, he remembered the name. He said a John Mathias used to live in Chicago and even as a kid was looked upon as a math prodigy. There were stories about him, like when he was four in nursery school. He was already playing with prime numbers (numbers that are divisible only by one and themselves, like 2, 3, 5, 7, 11, 13, 17 and so on). He asked his nursery teacher if she realized that no prime number could be the sum of two prime numbers unless one of them was 2 (like 19 being the sum of 2 and 17). And he told her he was counting up how many prime numbers could be summed in a single prime (like 31 being the sum of primes 3, 11 and 17). My professor recalled hearing that when John Mathias was five, he got into infinities. He asked his kindergarten teacher if one infinity could be smaller than another, like if you extend a natural number sequence to infinity, would just the even numbers of that sequence be a smaller infinity? That struck him as funny. Then at about the same age, so the legends

17

go, he somehow showed up at the University of Chicago math department claiming he figured out how to square the circle. That can't be done of course. No mathematician has ever been able to write an equation showing squares and circles with equal area. Mathias showed how it could be done with volume, i.e., in three dimensional shapes like square boxes and round balls. He was only five remember. According to my professor, what he did was take a milk carton and fill it with water to the point where the filled portion represented a perfect square. Then he poured that water into a balloon, squeezing it until it made a round ball. And it was true, here was a box and a ball with virtually the exact same volume of water. He argued that if you can square the volume of a ball, you can square the area of a circle. Of course he couldn't prove either mathematically, but for a five-year-old it made an impression.

He got his math degrees later at the same university, which is where my math prof heard about him. He said Mathias was remembered there as exceptionally brilliant and just as eccentric. He worked on a math theory of his own, something he called deconstructivism. My prof couldn't recall the details and apparently nobody took it seriously. It had something to do with collapsing dimensionality to a dimensionless point, to non-dimensionality. Like if you straighten out a bent line, what you're doing is to reduce the two dimensions that a bent line requires to the single dimension of a straight line. And a straight line is an extension, but what is it an extension of? An extensionless point? Mathias spent all his time puzzling over these things. He wanted to know if a point is extensionless, which is what a mathematical point is after all, how can this point be extended to become a line? To Mathias *the conundrum called for a mathematical big bang theory, extension coming from its very absence. My prof laughed and shrugged that no one in the department took any of this seriously, but Mathias certainly did, to his own professional detriment. He said he'd heard years back that Mathias wound up teaching in some prep school and that this school eventually had to let him go. There was never any scuttlebutt about him after that. My prof was amazed when I told him what happened. He found the whole thing very sad. A gifted man but a pointless life, he said. The irony of that observation got us both to laughing.*

To get back. After the cop talked to our math genius neighbor, things calmed down for a while, until the day of the grizzly event. I still can't get that strange woman out of my mind, the one involved. We'd only seen her twice before the tragedy. The first time in the lobby. My wife and I just came in from classes and saw this really striking figure waiting by the elevator. We wanted to greet her but she wouldn't look at us. When we got in she had already pressed our floor, six. Our elevator is the size of a closet so I had to stand just inches from her. I tried not to glance but what are you going to do next to someone with her looks. It's funny about that. Women, especially lookers, like to be seen but they don't like being looked at, not most of them. This one made you feel she didn't even want to be seen. My wife, bless her, tried conversation. She was going to be our neighbor after all. But that went nowhere. She glanced at my wife but all she gave us was a cold, quick, quarter smile, more like a nervous reflex. We let her off first. It was strange the way she slipped down the hall to her door, like someone there and yet not there. But it got stranger. The next time we saw her she was rushing past our door and

19

she had no hair. Hard to believe but she was completely bald. That spooked us out. We began to wonder what we'd done taking a flat on a floor filled with people like this.

Then, right after that, there was this sudden, tremendous crash of glass in the old guy's flat next to us. Later we found he had bashed a chair against a wall mirror, smashing it to pieces. The next thing we knew he had gone up to the roof. We could just make out his footsteps through the ceiling. The next time we saw either of these neighbors of ours again was six days later when we got back from classes and came upon the scene of the two of them in the hall, literally drenched in blood.

The writings of his that I place next were done in the days leading up to that event. It's quite poignant, and the last piece of this writing winds up being pretty mystical, or maybe deranged is the better word. Not too coherent anyway to an engineer's mind. It has to be included, however, if his story is to be told in full, which I think it deserves to be. So here it is.

*   *   *

It was always my intention to spend the last five days up on the roof, as I am now doing. But I never thought about what the weather could be like when I set this time 4995 days ago. It's into the fall and getting cold, though thankfully not yet unbearable up here, so far at least. Right now it's overcast and threatening rain, the kind of sky I have come to prefer. I'm wearing two undershirts, two top shirts and a wool sweater, leaning against a huge pigeon hutch some tenant put up ages ago. The pigeons behind me didn't like having me here, but they've calmed down and are quiet now. Again, why do I bother bringing you in on this? Perhaps, if nothing else, to satisfy my ironic streak. Whoever you are, you will be reading this after I have ceased to be, and you will confirm that it's so, making my negation doubly true: *he who never lived no longer lives.* That's a double negative, paradoxically, which is the extent of what I've wound up being, or not being. Sometimes I feel even the pigeons here are laughing at me.

I want to explain about the roof, why the roof. If you go to the back of the building and look down, you would see an earthen excavation six floors below. A shallow pit, dug out for who knows what reason and then apparently abandoned. Perhaps it was the beginnings of a drainage field years ago, before the city sewers reached this far. I came up on the roof and spotted this earthen hole the day I arrived. What caught my eye was the excavation's shape, almost perfectly circular, like *naught*. And close to the building. If you leaned over and dropped something, you'd hit the *zero* dead center. That's is exactly what I did ten minutes ago with the key to my flat. And then did the same with my shoes. I threw these things over so I can't go back even if I wanted to. I can't go anywhere. I am fixed here on this roof, with no money, no identification, no food, nothing but the things I'm wearing. If you add *zero* to *zero,* you know what you get. I suppose some might say you get what you deserve.

I wish to clarify a point. It's not despair that drives me to this. Yes, I am on edge, I cannot deny that, but I am not in any way depressed. I know that

21

many are led to take their lives because of some overwhelming humiliation or unbearable loss. That's not my case. No, the cause with me is logic, the logic of descending numbers as they approach their limit. You see, when I was young, everyone took me for a numbers prodigy and I think probably I was. But nothing good came of it, not ever, and nothing ever will. Take away one from 5000 for 4995 consecutive days and where does that leave you? On a roof. And where does the logic of descending numbers lead, I ask you, if not to its limit, if not to *zero*. You can divide a number an infinite number of ways and never get to zero, but subtraction can get you there in a single operation.

It is almost noon of day *five*. Eleven seventeen a.m. to be exact. As I compute it, all of 6499 minutes remain to my life. That large number makes the *zero* point seem distant still. That final moment as yet has little reality for me. But I am under no illusion. The last minutes will not be easy. Not like it was back then, fixing the *day* so far in advance it was just an abstraction, an idea of something that would happen one far-off day in the future, like anyone's eventual death. Yes, back then, when I was living in the subways, I played with thoughts of a quick finish. I stood on station platforms more than once staring at the tracks as trains came thundering in. Others have leaped, but for every one who did, how many never got beyond the thought. I was one of those, always walking away asking myself, *does it have to be now?* Yes, I had made my decision, I saw the logic, but where was the rush?

Then I found this vacant building with this flat just under the roof and I took it as a sign. I could bide my time. I elected for lots of it, for 5000 days, a nice, round number so far off in the future it let me breathe again. I had no problem justifying the delay. After all, the method and timing were immovably fixed. There was no longer any question about the how or when. And so, with time on my hands, I could settle in and maybe still do some work. I was having it both ways, as you can doubtless see.

And I did do some things. During the long holiday I worked on my deconstructivist conjecture and on some conjectures of others, some famous ones, like trying to prove the Goldman Conjecture about prime numbers. As with everything else, these efforts came to nothing. But I will never lose my fascination with numbers. You know by now, I'm sure, that my digit of choice is *zero*. There'd be no serious mathematics without it. Of course zero can't be a *digit*, not literally, but what intrigues me is whether *zero* is even a number. Numbers stand for quantities. How can *nothing* be counted? You can't add *zero* to anything, or subtract *zero* from anything. You can't multiply by *zero* or divide by *zero*. Interestingly though, like I just said, the one mathematical operation that allows for zero is subtraction. Five take away five gives you *zero*. John Mathias take away John Mathias gives you *zero*. So what is *zero*? The irony is no one who finds out can tell you.

Day *four*. I've spent today in a stew of mixed feelings, anticipating the *day*, the scheduled moment when this ragged bag of memories mercifully gets emptied. Yes, to be sure, I'm on edge, excited even, awaiting its approach, and to be honest not a little apprehensive as the hours slip away. The last steps will not be a cakewalk. Nor is the rain now helping my frame of mind. It's been drizzling all day, a fine cold rain, cooping me up inside this hutch, unable to stand. The pigeons aren't happy having me inside their home. I'm the intruder now. There's irony for you.

Day *three*. Is it so that there is really only one way you are meant to be, one work you are meant to do, one final love you are meant to have? Doesn't God (if there is one) have a plan B for wayward souls? Can one never start over? Pick up where one left off? Does one even want to? I try not to think of her but in these last hours her sweet, tender face will not leave me. She used to call me *her Johnny. Johnny,* she'd say, *how happy we will be.* I hear her say that over and again, but what would it have been like? Would my fear of suffocation ever go away? How many kids would I have had to put to bed at night, correct their misbehavior, bandage their cuts? Could I have learned to be a father? And my work, would it have been blessed perhaps, even to the Fields Medal I fantasized about? And the pregnancy. By now she'd be a young woman almost. What name was she given? Does she look like Carrie, have my gift for math? Would she ever think of me? Why do I think it would have been a girl?

I fight these thoughts. They plague me. Yes, my

Carrie would have meant a neat, comfortable home, hot meals, a warm bed, and lots of gentle laughter, on her part at least. But it would have been replete, yes replete with rosaries, and incense and bells all for the sake of a Bloody Cross. What does any of that have to do with me, with this roof, this bothersome rain, with this moth bag of thoughts and feelings I live with? The worst are *regrets*. Let me say it again, I will never give in to them.

Day *two*. It is exactly noon. I hear a distant church bell. Just 36 hours, 2160 minutes to midnight when in the very next second, Day *one* leaps to *zero*. I leave the thought at that. The incessant rain has me cooped up with these pigeons. They will never accept my being here. I don't think I can write more. I've said what I have to say. I ask you to forgive me but I'm not even sure for what.

Day *one*. I don't know what to make of this but I feel it's worth recording. Minutes ago someone came up on the roof, a woman. It's already dusk and still raining and I couldn't make out the face as she passed me where I'm crouched in the hutch. She had a raincoat on and a hat pulled over the head. Oddly she seemed not to have hair. For some reason I'm almost certain she is the silent one who came on my floor. I watched as she went over to the roof edge, right at my spot, and looked down. She stood that way for quite some time and then she slid down with her back against the parapet, facing my direction. She had no idea someone was observing her. She seemed fairly young, and even in the failing light there was something quite remarkable about her. What she was doing on the roof was her business, but as far I was concerned I wanted her out of here. For the next seven hours this roof has to be for me alone, me and these pigeons. The pigeons actually gave me an idea. With an abrupt swish of both hands I excited the birds, getting them to fly out in a flurry of wings. The sudden eruption startled her and got her up on her feet. Maybe she sensed a presence. Whatever, in the next instant she went below and I had what I wanted.

Even the pigeons have fled.

One hour to zero. Goodbye my reader, whoever you are. Say a prayer for me if you're the type. I'm frankly afraid now. Who knows what awaits on the far side of *zero*. Do positive numbers descend to *zero* only for *zero* to usher in the negatives, negative numbers stretching to infinity? What is infinite negation? Will I soon find out? Yes, this is the risk. But Mathias the Math Freak has made his bed. What was set up years ago must be done. Besides, what is here to keep me? Carrie, I tried. You know it's true. I am so sorry I could not be for you. I trust by now you've forgotten me. And that before you forgot me, you forgave. It will be easier for me to believe that. Somehow I think you have. Goodbye Carrie, to you most especially, my once and only friend. We came so close.

I have to stop. If what I do next is wrong, may I find forgiveness.

* * *

*We heard the elevator arrive on our floor, and then him
opening the door to his flat, just as my wife and I went to
bed late that night, not long after midnight. We heard him
through the walls sweeping up glass. When we went out
early the next morning for classes, we found another of his
cans of beans. But it was very different this time. The can
was unopened. We both figured it was meant to be a sign of
peace, and all the way to school we talked about how maybe
we should have him in for supper or something, try making
friends with him.*

*We came back later that morning, maybe just in time
to save a life. Even in the elevator as it approached the
sixth floor, we could smell the gas. When we stepped out
the fumes almost overwhelmed us. It's a mercy neither of
us are smokers. Before I relate what confronted us at the far
end of the hall, let me include his last remarks, things he
had to have written that very night after he came down
from the roof. You need to have this to complete the picture.*

* * *

Yes, I was standing on the edge of the parapet. Despite my shaky legs I somehow got myself up on it.
The rain had stopped (and there was even a moon)
but the parapet surface was still treacherously wet.
Even these last seconds had their irony, with me
exercising considerable care to balance myself to be
sure not to slip. It was seconds past midnight on day
zero and the final moment had come. As I stared down
at the excavation six floors below, readying myself,
gathering my will, something extraordinary took

place before my eyes. The dark circle yawned open to become the entrance to a black, endless tunnel. From that blackness I felt a powerful force reach up, pulling me, wanting to draw me down. The vision or whatever it was horrified me and I felt myself waver. Seconds passed. Was I not to do what I had promised myself every day for the past 5000? Then voices began to scream up at me, *Come on, you know your time has come. Do it! Just do it!* Faces suddenly appeared, glaring up at me, vacant, lifeless faces with eyes like shattered glass, some without eyes at all, myriads of faces. *Come, join us, you belong with us here.* Then, from still deeper within, waves of hideous, sneering voices screaming up at me. *See, Mathias the Math Freak is afraid. He's just a coward, afraid to do the one thing he promised himself. The one thing he promised us.* Waves of mocking laughter reached up to sweep me off the parapet.

I was held back for a second by a fleeting image of Carrie, my Carrie, a Carrie alas no longer young, her face lined with sorrows, her eyes staring up at me, transfixed in a look of utter horror. For that one brief moment the din subsided but in an instant she was gone and the roar flooded back. *She's gone for you,* the voices screamed in ghoulish glee, *you threw her away. Now do the same for yourself. What are you waiting for? Remember the logic. The logic of zero, of nothing, of zilch! Do it now! Leap! Leap! Leap!*

Then, as I drew myself up, steeling myself to obey the inexorable logic of my own making, in that very instant the howling abruptly ceased. The horrific laughter was silenced and a great quiet settled over the blackness six floors below. Across the entrance to that blackness the bloody figure of a man came into focus. His entire body was lacerated, crimson with wounds, and he gave the appearance of being close to death. But, incredibly, he stretched out two arms, one to each side as if barring my way. He looked up at me, a long, steady gaze with eyes I shall never, ever forget. When he spoke the words, I knew, I understood who he was. *Everything is forgiven, Johnny, everything. Go, save yourself.* Then just as suddenly he disappeared, and six floors below there was nothing but an ordinary, shallow excavation situated at the base of the building. And, in the dim light of the moon, something in that circle that looked like a pair of shoes. I needed to go get them. I might mention that the pigeons came circling back as well.

He called me *Johnny*, just the way Carrie did. How long has it been since anyone spoke my name like that? I wonder if. . . .

These were the last words John Mathias ever wrote. We figured he broke off in the middle of that last sentence the moment he smelled the gas. We don't know for certain of course exactly how things went, but here's what we've pieced together based on all the evidence.

He smelled gas and went out into the hall. He realized it was coming from that woman's flat on the other side of him. How he managed to break down her door is a mystery given how frail this guy was. Once inside he must have gone right to the stove and turned off the jets. Then he dragged her out into the hall and with his shoe broke the hall window to get air. That's how he cut himself and why there was so much

29

blood. His wrist was deeply gashed and blood was still spilling over him when we got there, and over the woman and the floor and broken glass. He was holding her, bending close, barely getting out these few words he kept repeating, "Don't go there. O lady, don't go there." We couldn't tell if she was still alive at that point. Soon as we saw what had happened, my wife rushed down for help (none of us has phones). I separated them and applied a tourniquet to his arm to stop the bleeding. I then half lifted, half dragged him into his flat (his door was wide open) and I stretched him out on his bed. He was unconscious by now. Then I went out to the woman and literally carried her to our flat and laid her out on the floor in the kitchen and threw open the window. There was still a faint pulse. When my wife got back she put a pillow under the woman's head and wiped off blood as best she could. I myself went back to the old man. I found him with rapid shallow breaths. It didn't look like he was going to make it. By the time the medics finally got here, he was gone. They took them both off in gurneys. The woman herself was just barely alive. We hadn't thought to ask where they were bringing her, so we never did find out what happened, whether she survived. We were sorry about that because it would have been quite interesting to know who in the world this woman was. She seemed so out of the ordinary. For some reason, though, we think she must have pulled through.

I have to tell you something else before leaving off this account. As I said earlier, the landlord agreed to let us clean up the two flats in exchange for one month's break in our rent. It turned out that neither flat needed much attention. All we found in hers was her purse and some pathetic few items of clothing. We gave the purse to the police. I did look in it though. She had a weird Polish last name I can't remember now. Her first name as I recall was Monica.

The old guy kept his place pretty clean, and anyway he had very little in it. His shelves were bare, his refrigerator was empty. The can of beans that he left at our door the morning of the tragedy was the last bit of food he had. As I recall now, even the bed I laid him on had been neatly made. But several things are worth mentioning. One was that all the earlier notes he had written previously were ripped up and scattered all over the floor. As I mentioned before, we had quite a task piecing them together, like a jigsaw puzzle. The last note he wrote, however, the one I included just above, was found with his few books and items of clothing all stacked on the kitchen table. The clothes had been carefully folded. This little assemblage was everything he owned. It looked as if he were getting ready to leave the place and take these things with him. But on top of that little pile was the most interesting find of all. An envelope with just the name Carrie on it, printed in big letters. Carrie, the girl he made pregnant years before and then walked away from. The letter was sealed, and do you know, neither my wife nor I felt we could open it. Not that we weren't plenty tempted, but whatever he wrote to this Carrie, we decided, was his business and not ours. Tempting, but we have since honored that decision. We keep it unopened along with the unopened can of beans, in honor of his memory. You know, all in all, he wasn't such a bad guy, not after what he did at the end.

TRUE OR FALSE

THE PRIESTS AT ST. ANDREWS were in the habit of hearing confessions before the 5:30 Mass on Saturday, though not every Saturday the way it was in former times. Hardly anyone now ever came except old ladies who used to belong to the Altar Society, and very occasionally a parishioner with some sort of real problem, usually of a domestic turn not having anything to do with serious sin exactly. And sometimes a stranger would enter the confessional, someone whose voice the priest had never heard before, someone perhaps from a neighboring parish hoping for anonymity. These cases would generally involve something more recognizable as sin.

Given all this, Father Louis Reilly, pastor of St. Andrews, decided, reluctantly enough, that confessions need only be heard before the 5:30 every other Saturday. His young assistant, Father Timothy O'Brien, the parochial vicar, certainly had no problem with this arrangement. People with a pressing problem on those off-Saturdays can always call the rectory and make an appointment.

That's just what happened on one of those Saturdays. It was close to five o'clock and Father Louis, who had the 5:30 that Saturday, was in his study with the door closed. Father Tim was already dressed in sweater and jeans for an evening out and was about to leave when the phone rang.

"Confessions are held on the first and third Saturdays," he said when he heard the reason for the call.

"To tell you the truth I really don't know if any of the parishes are hearing confessions today," he answered pleasantly, his foot up on the desk. "Probably not this late," he added, noticing a spot of something on his new Reeboks.

"Well, it is pretty late now," Father Tim said looking at his watch.

"No!" he said laughing. "We don't hear confessions over the telephone. That's one thing we can't do, at least not yet!" He laughed again.

"Well," he said, "is it something that can't really wait? How about tomorrow before Mass maybe?"

"No, sure, fine. No, hey it's OK," he said, his voice masking a sour look. "Are you nearby?"

"All right, just come to the rectory," he said. "I'm Father Tim. I'll be here."

He hung up and immediately dialed another number.

"Joe," he said, "I've gotten tied up here for a bit. No, I don't think so. Maybe ten, twenty minutes tops. If it's more than that, you guys go ahead. I'll catch up with you at the restaurant. Save some calamari for me!" he added with a laugh and hung up.

A thick-set, blue-collar gent in his early forties

33

arrived ten minutes later, looking rather glum. "Shall we go into my office?" Father Tim asked, pointing to a door. "Or we could go over to the confessional in the church. Suit yourself. We still have time before the 5:30."

"This is OK," the penitent said, moving to the office.

"I haven't been to confession for a while," the man said when they were seated.

"That's no problem," Father Tim said with a wave of his hand. He liked to get people to relax.

"It's been a real long while," the man said.

"Well, how long?"

"About twenty years, maybe longer," he said.

Father Tim said with a nod, "At least you're here now. That's good."

"We're supposed to go once a year, isn't that right?" the man asked.

"Yes," Father Tim said. "Not a bad idea. Gets things off your chest. You married?"

"Yeah," he said.

"So," Father Tim said, shifting, "what's on your mind?"

I'd like to go to confession," the man repeated.

"Right,." Father Tim hesitated. He noticed the man was staring at his Reeboks. "Let me get my stole." He got up and rummaged through a closet. "It's in here somewhere," he said absently. After a bit, he suddenly stopped. "Ah," he said, hitting his hand to his head, "my bedroom closet. Be right back."

A minute later he returned.

"So now," Father Tim said slipping back into his seat, his purple stole slung incongruously down around a blue-green sweater over a green turtle-neck. "Shall we begin?" he gestured when the man didn't say anything.

"Help me out, Father," the man said at length. "It's been so long. Isn't there something special I'm supposed to say to get this started?"

"Well," Father Tim said with an effort to smile, "you usually tell the priest how long it's been since your last confession. But you've already done that."

The man sat forward a little. "I remember it," he said, his face brightening with a smile. "Bless me, Father, for I have sinned. It's been twenty years since my last confession."

"Very good," said Father Tim. "Just go ahead now. Tell me what's bothering you."

"I don't know how to say this, Father," the man said. "It's hard for me."

"Well, something is bothering you, right?"

"Yes, Father, definitely."

"Can you tell me what it is?"

"That's just it, Father. I'm having trouble finding the words."

"Have you committed some sin?"

"Like fornication, Father?"

"Fornication, whatever."

"Not really, Father. I don't screw around or any-thing like that. I look at the girls at the plant once in a while maybe the way I shouldn't, but not real-ly. I mean I don't do things with them in my mind,

35

like. You know what I mean? Maybe I used to but I'm past that sort of stuff now. Getting too old for one thing."

"You said you're married?"

"Yes, Father."

"Well, is everything all right there? Are you fighting with your wife?"

"Nah, we hardly talk to each other. I mean we get along OK. She stays in her corner. I stay in mine. I'm married almost twenty years, Father. I've already said everything I'm gonna say to her probably a hundred times over."

"Well, where does it hurt, like the doctor said. Something's bothering you, it seems."

"What's sin, Father?"

Father Tim blinked and tried not to smile. "That's a good question actually," he said. "I often ponder that myself," he added with a laugh.

"Sin is you go against the Ten Commandments, right?"

"That's a good place to start," Father Tim said.

"I don't steal, I don't really lie much, I don't hurt anybody, I don't fornicate. Does that mean I'm not a sinner?"

"Hey, I'm just a priest, not a judge. That's the job of your conscience. I can see that something's bothering you."

"Yeah, but I can't put my finger on it exactly. I thought maybe you could help me."

Father Tim hesitated for a moment. "Sin," he said, "is something you do that is against your own best interests. That's the bottom line. You sin when you do something that hurts you yourself, the inner you."

"What about others, what about God, Father?"

"Well, when you sin against others, you hurt them, but who are you really hurting? You hurt yourself. You can't hurt God, right? If you cheat on your wife or something like that, who's getting hurt the most in the final analysis, you or her? You. You hurt the relationship. You destroy your right to that relationship. That's the bottom line far as I can see."

"What if you kill somebody? It's the other person dies, not you."

"Well, you can take a person's life but not his soul. But a person who does that could be destroying his own soul."

"I see what you're getting at, Father. Maybe that's what's bothering me." He paused for a moment and then asked, "Do you have a Bible, Father?"

"I have one right here, as a matter of fact," the priest said taking one from his desk.

"Could I see it, Father?" the man said.

The priest handed him the Bible.

"Father, I never read this thing but the other day I picked it up and just started with the first page. I read about Adam and Eve and the garden, you know." The man leaned forward. "They committed the first sin, right?" he asked.

"We don't know exactly," the priest said. "It's a story meant for our instruction."

"A story, Father?" The man asked. "You're saying none of this happened? I think you're wrong there, Father. It happened. It says so right here."

Father Tim looked at his watch. "You know," he said, "you've caught me at a bad time. I was just on my way out. We could talk about this some other time."

The man seemed not to hear. "And there's this tree in the middle of the garden," he continued. He had opened the Bible and was pointing to a page in the early chapters of *Genesis*.

"The tree of the knowledge of good and evil," the priest said mechanically.

"Yeah, that one too. But this other tree, in the exact middle of the garden, Father, the tree of life. What's that all about, Father?"

"You know we should talk about this some other time," Father Tim said making as if to stand.

"And after they sinned," the man went on, "God puts this angel in front of the tree with a flaming sword so nobody can get at it. Why'd he do that, Father? Isn't God supposed to be a good guy? I mean everybody else does things like that to protect their turf, but why God? He's supposed to love us, right?"

"Look," the priest said more severely, "I really have to go."

"Just let me get this off my chest, OK, Father?"

"OK, sure," Father Tim said after a moment's hesitation, recovering his sense of priestly duty. "No problem." He sank back in his chair and reflected for a moment. "The tree of life is a figure of speech, I suppose," he said to the man. "The writer had to explain the presence of death in a world that God created and said was good."

"So he puts that flaming sword there so we couldn't eat the apples or whatever from that tree, so that we would die? Is that the idea?"

"Well, there's got to be some connection between sin and death," Father Tim said, trying to hold his own interest. "This is pretty abstract stuff. Is this what you came to see me about?"

"No, Father. I just wondered about it. Like there's something missing in my life. Maybe God's just blocking it off from me."

"What do you mean by 'it' ?"

"Life, Father. Real life. You know what I mean? Half the time I feel like something that's gone sour in the fridge, like I been just rotting away most of my life. I never seen nothing, nothing you could really call life. Did you ever think we're all rottin' apples? Know what I mean?"

"I'm not sure I follow you exactly," the priest said.

"Well, Father, take today. I get up at seven. I eat breakfast. My wife doesn't talk to me except to remind me to take out the garbage. The kids are fighting. I start out the day yelling. My wife makes a face and goes upstairs. I have to make my own sandwich. And this is supposed to be my home. A man's home, you know?" The man shook his head at this point. "I can't even take the couple of dollars to buy a sandwich 'cause I got to replace the roof this year and there's no way I'm gonna be able to do that."

"Where do you work?" The priest asked, hoping to move the conversation along.

"You mean where *did* I work," the man said.

"You're unemployed?"

"I lost my job today."

"You got laid off?"

"I got fired. I called my boss a stupid jerk. Something worse actually."

"You know this isn't exactly a confessional matter." The priest looked at his watch and stood up. "You need to talk to somebody who can help you with these problems."

"I need absolution, Father."

The priest stood there for a moment looking at him. The man was bent over, plowing callused fingers through thick, rough hair just beginning to gray around the edges. "What have you done?" The priest asked at length.

The man looked up at the priest and gave him a strange smile. He picked up the Bible and flipped to the back. "Here, Father. In the last chapter of the Bible, in the book of Revelations, Christ is talking about this tree again, the tree of life. The same tree. It's the first time we hear of it since *Genesis*. I looked. It ain't nowhere else in the Bible I could see. It's in *Genesis*, right at the beginning of the Bible and it comes up again on the very last page. It ain't anyplace else. Just at the beginning and end, right?"

"I'm not really sure."

"Believe me, Father. I went through it last night. It's at the beginning and at the end, so it's got to be pretty important, right Father?"

The priest sat down again and was peering at the man. "I have to go," he said quietly. "If you want to talk about these things we can do it some other time. Make an appointment. I'd be happy to chat with you."

"I'll tell you what I think, Father," the man said,

oblivious to the priest's impatience. "Look, here's what Jesus said. He says he's the beginning and the end, and that he's coming soon and he's going to pay every man for what he's done. But he says the ones who wash their robes will be able to eat from the tree of life and enter the new city by the gates. You read it too, right, Father?" He asked, handing the priest the Bible.

The priest took the Bible and looked at the passage. "Right there, Father," the man said, getting up from his seat and pointing at the passage in question. "Ain't that something? There's gonna be this new Jerusalem that will come right down from heaven, all shining with diamonds and precious jewels and stuff. It looks like the angel is still there guarding everything but now he lets certain people through. These are the good guys, the ones who cleaned up their act. They can walk right in and eat that tree all they want."

He sat down and shook his head. Neither of them moved for a time and then the man said to the priest. "Any of this make sense to you, Father?" The priest looked at him curiously and said nothing.

"Let me have that for a moment, will you, Father?" The man said, reaching for the Bible. "Here's the other side of the story. It says that certain kinds of people will be kept out. That angel ain't gonna let them in." He began to read. "'Outside are the dogs and sorcerers and fornicators and murderers and idolaters...'." The man stopped reading and looked up. "No problem for us there, right, Father?" he said with a wink and a smile.

The priest just looked at him and said nothing.

"But here's this other thing, Father. This is the part that gets to me. Those who have led a 'false life' will also be kept outside, along with the dogs and fornicators." The man studied the priest. "What's that mean to you, Father? A false life."

The priest blinked and started to say something but stopped. "It could mean a number of things," he said after a moment.

"Anyway, Father, can I have your absolution?"

"Surely, but you have to tell me some sin first, OK?" The priest said.

"I just did."

"What sin was that?" the priest said.

"A false life, Father. That's me. I've been living a false life. I'm one of those guys."

"OK. Right. But can you be a little more specific? False in what way?"

"I'll be specific, Father. My life stinks. Lately I look at myself when I'm shaving and want to throw up." He rubbed his hand across his chin. "I'll give you details, Father. I get up in the morning. It starts there. I go to work, glad to get out of the house. I get to the plant and wonder how there could be such stupid people in the world. I'm talking about my ex-boss. Lunch time I throw my dumb sandwich away and spend five dollars I don't have on a beer and a plate of spaghetti at a diner down the street from the plant. In the afternoon my boss tells me I didn't do something the way he said and I tell him, it was dumb to do it that way. He tells me I'm going to do it his way anyway, and I tell him he has his head up . . . you know where."

42

"So it's your anger that bothers you?"

"Naw, I wasn't angry. I was just mad. He was partly right you know. I knew that. I didn't like him coming up to me that way, that's all."

"So you want to confess a sin of pride?"

"Father, I want to confess I been living a false life. That's my sin. I can see it."

"I'm having trouble with what you mean by a false life."

"I just told you Father — *my* life.

Father Tim's gaze began to drift past the man.

"Father," the man pushed on, "Do you believe there is such a thing as this tree of life."

"Sure. As a figure of speech, I guess I do."

"Do you think that 'figure' or whatever you call it, is going to be for you?"

"I certainly hope so."

"Me too," he said. "So how about it, Father?"

The priest looked at him uncertainly.

"Absolution, Father, absolution."

The priest, seeking some definite matter he could legitimately absolve, asked the man, "You're sorry for the sins of your past life, correct?"

"You bet, Father."

"What about anger?"

"Anger, everything, Father. The whole kit and caboodle."

The priest smiled, hesitated an instant, then raised his hand and began to recite the words of absolution.

The man interrupted him at once. "Father, excuse me. Don't I have to make an act of contrition? I want to do this right."

"If you wish. My feeling is that just your coming in here is an act of contrition."

"I'd like to do this the way I was taught as a kid, Father. But I don't remember how it goes."

"Just tell God you are sorry. That will be enough."

The man hesitated. "OK, Father, if you say so." He knelt down in front of the priest and began to pray. "I'm sorry, Lord. I'm sorry for being a phony, for living what you call a false life. Lord, forgive me. Jesus, help me to be different. Give me a real life."

"OK, that's good," the priest said. He recited the words of absolution, making the sign of the cross.

"I think God is pleased with you," he said, putting his hand on the man's shoulder.

"I'm clean," the man said with a broad smile. "It's been twenty years."

Father Tim helped the penitent get up. "God bless you," he said.

They each turned away and made separate moves to depart. The priest thoughtfully folded up his stole and placed it carefully on the desk. The man, his face all shiny, was on his way out when he stopped and turned back to the priest. "Father," he said. "There's something at the end of the Bible could be for you too." He picked up the book from the priest's desk and pointed to a particular verse. "Read this sometime, Father," he said, thumping his finger on the page. "Maybe it's got your number."

They left, the penitent to his new life, the priest to Luigi's and his calamari. But the confession the priest heard stuck with him. He was uncharacteristically quiet that evening with his friends. They asked him if anything was wrong. He laughed it off, but he wasn't his usual cut-up self. When they broke up and he was back at the rectory later that night, he went into his office and got the Bible. Before turning out his light, he turned to the book of *Revelation* and looked up the passage he had been told had his number. It was virtually the last lines of Scripture, a sort of postscript the Apostle had written to warn his readers.

"This is my solemn attestation to all who hear the prophesies in this book: if anyone adds anything to them, God will add to him every plague mentioned in this book; if anyone cuts anything out of the prophesies of this book, God will cut out his share of the tree of life and the holy city which are described in this book. The one who attests to these things says: I am indeed coming soon."

Father Tim read it twice. Was the passage supposed to be about him? Was he one of those who added anything to the prophesies? Had he cut out anything? He didn't see it that way but the priest did not sleep well that night. His thoughts kept going back over his life. Was it a good life? Was his possibly a false life also? How many times had he mocked his superiors? Not in so many words perhaps. How long had it been since he had been to confession? He, a priest of God.

The following week was not a good week for Father Tim. "You all right, Tim?" Father Louis asked him one morning, observing the younger priest over the top edge of his newspaper. The pastor liked his assistant but they never seemed to really connect. Different generations, different wave lengths. It made the older pastor a little sad.

"I'm fine," Father Tim lied.

"Sure? You look a little wan."

"No, everything's great. Guess I'm tired." He poured himself another cup of coffee.

"I can take the funeral this morning if you want," the pastor said.

"Thanks," Father Tim said, shaking his head and smiling. "I'm OK. Funerals aren't my thing," he added after a time.

The older priest, back into his newspaper, looked over at his assistant for a second, made a sound in his throat and went back to his reading.

"But that's what I'm here for," Father Tim said absently. He got up and went down the hall to his room.

The funeral was for a middle-aged woman who had died of cancer. Someone from the old neighborhood surrounding the church. She never came to St. Andrew's far as he knew. She had three children living and they all had kids. Her oldest boy was killed in Iraq. Father Tim saw someone in the pews who must have been the husband, along with what looked like scads of uncles and aunts, siblings, cousins and kids of all ages. There was a really old lady that could have been the grandmother. The deceased woman must have been loved. Probably a terrific cook. A big woman in a big lively family like in the old days. The kind they don't grow anymore.

"She was a good woman," Father Tim heard himself saying from the pulpit. "She lived a good life." He usually said that even if he knew nothing about the deceased. He could tell from the faces of the surviving family what kind of life the dead person had lived. Once he got into it he knew he liked to preach. He liked reaching people. For him the homilies at Mass were more important, more real than the Sacrament. The church is people not sacraments, one of his seminary professors used to say and he couldn't agree more. But today the words he was speaking seemed to him to just fall flat. They left a bad taste in his mouth. What was going wrong with him?

At the cemetery after the interment, one of the family members came up to him. An uncle probably. Father Tim recognized his face. Back of the church at the seven-thirty Mass Sunday mornings. Sometimes he ushered. The parishioner kept shaking his head as he told the priest about her end. "She wouldn't see anybody, Father," he said. "She was angry for a long time. At the end I think she was just scared. She should have seen a priest. She didn't have the last rites, nothing."

"Wasn't she a good woman?" Father Tim asked.

"She was OK, Father, don't get me wrong. But she wasn't a happy person, know what I mean?"

"Seems like a good family," the priest said.

"We got our share of problems, Father. Don't you kid yourself. People ain't themselves at funerals, know what I mean?"

"I suppose you're right."

"Pray for her, will you? And while you're at it, do me a favor, Father, and mention my name too, OK? I'm Anthony."

"Of course," Father Tim said. "Anthony." He had already forgotten the name of the deceased woman.

By the end of the week, Father Tim had a bad cold and headache that would not go away.

"I'll take the morning Mass," Father Louis said at breakfast. It was Saturday and there was only the nine o'clock. "You go back to bed. Get some rest."

Father Louis took confessions that afternoon. It was the young curate's turn but Father Louis insisted. One of the altar ladies was already there waiting for him at four o'clock. She was there every month. The trouble this time was her daughter-in-law yelled at her and she gave it to her right back. It took all of about three minutes to get this off her chest and be absolved. After her there was no one, not for forty minutes. Father Louis sat there in the reconciliation room and read his office. He didn't mind the solitude. It was a pleasant little room. The late afternoon sun shone behind a small stained glass window, creating a lovely colored rainbow effect. The air in the room seemed liquid with colors. There was an empty chair for the penitent to sit facing him, and a chair behind a screen if the penitent needed privacy. Every few minutes Father Louis turned the page of his breviary. He'd read a few lines and then close his eyes. Sometimes he couldn't tell if it was prayer or sleep. He felt at peace in a world he knew wasn't peaceful any more.

He must have been dozing just before the hour was up when the door to the confessional which was left ajar opened wide. Father Tim was standing before him, looking forlorn and crumpled. Father Louis looked up at him. "Tim," he said. "What's up?"

Father Tim exhaled a huge volume of air in a painful sigh and sat down heavily on the chair facing his boss. "This has been hell week," he said, shaking his head.

Father Louis studied him for a moment. "Cold any better?"

"I'm in some kind of hole," Father Tim said. "I need something to get me out of this funk."

"Want to talk?" Father Louis asked, putting down his breviary.

Father Tim shook his head and looked at his boss. "I haven't been to confession for three years," he said meekly.

Father Louis raised his eyebrows and nodded. "That's too long," he said.

"Someone came in for confession last Saturday," Father Tim said. "He hadn't been to confession for twenty years. When he left with the absolution, he was like a new man. It was beautiful."

Father Louis nodded and waited.

Father Tim looked at his boss with a kind of lame smile, leaned forward putting his head into his hands and began speaking to the floor. "You and I kind of keep to ourselves," he said. "We don't talk much. Maybe we should. We sort of like . . . stay in our own corners." He looked up at his boss. A soft light had crept into the eyes of the older priest. The colored light coming through the stained glass window had painted his face in soft liquid hues. The old priest's face seemed to be glowing. They sat looking at each other in the silence of the little room for an interminable minute. Then the young priest slid to his knees.

"Bless me, Father, for I have sinned. It's been a whole lifetime since my last confession . . . "

Here's Mashed

Roger had been called a lot of things in his day, things he usually took in his stride being good-natured. But last night when his girl and maybe one-day-wife-to-be Marjori called him *stupid ridiculous*, that did it. It was said in the heat of battle, but even so, this was going too far. She said other things too, but *stupid ridiculous* was definitely the last straw. And it wasn't the first time she called him stupid. "Who does she think she is?" he told his buddy George in the plant cafeteria the day after this latest blow-up. "You wouldn't say something like that to a dog," he said as he walked down the line, pointing out a particular chicken breast to the lady behind the counter. And he wanted a double helping of mashed potatoes. Things were sure not working out between him and her. No sir, not anymore.

"We've been going steady for seven years and engaged for two," he said digging into his meal.

"That's the trouble," his friend George told him. "You know each other too well."

But Roger was on a different track. "You don't know how much I spent on her. Just the meals alone," he said picking up the breast. "I don't want to tell you. It'd break your heart."

"Yeah," George said, "you should be glad you've found out before it was too late." George always saw things in broad daylight. "Try and get the ring back," he advised.

Just as they'd been doing for some years now, Roger and Marjori met for dinner the next week, this time at Joe's Westside Steak House. It was a little more expensive but Roger liked to play the big man now and then, even in the present circumstances. Marjori, who to her mother's annoyance spelled her name with an "i" no matter what the baptismal certificate said, was a little late that night. She was usually always a little late now that Roger thought about it. Roger sat waiting for her at a table way in the back where it was dimly lit and more private. He ordered a shot with a beer chaser and then another. She wasn't going to treat him like a doormat, that's for sure.

Marjori came in all business, like nothing ever happened. And Roger despite himself jumped up and took the cheek she half-offered. Marjori didn't go for public pecking. And anyway real necking was for later in the car in front of her house with the single light her mother left burning, when nobody could care less about the lipstick smears on somebody's face. Marjori looked pretty good tonight, Roger had to admit. She was not what you would call a great looker exactly. Maybe she was a little pudgy in the face like George said, but she had something going for her all the same. Roger liked them with a little meat on. They sat facing each other and Marjori, acting like everything was just rosy between them, told him all about her day.

That was the usual routine, Marjori talking about her day. Roger knew all the people at her work, knew their habits, their quirks, their hang-ups, which of the guys were cute, like this whats-his-name in Purchasing, and which were real losers, like her boss. He didn't mind her going on because it made her happy to unload like that while they ate. Tonight it was her boss again, her all-time favorite subject. Something he said today was really uncalled for, something to make a decent person blush, she said. When Roger suggested that maybe she should say something to him, you know, like tell him to wash his mouth out, she said don't be ridiculous. And that did it.

Roger decided now he was definitely going to do what he had decided earlier, which was to lay it right out on the table, once and for all. Enough is enough.

"Listen, Marjori," he said, "I don't like it when you call me those names."

"What?" she said.

"You heard me."

"Don't be ridiculous," she said. "That really is stupid."

"I said I don't want you to call me that."

"It's just an expression," she said with a face.

"Well, I don't like it and I don't want you to do it anymore."

"Don't be silly," she said. She picked up the menu. As far as she was concerned the topic was food.

"Look," Roger said, "we had a big fight the other night, remember?"

She looked up from the menu at him.

"You said I was stupid ridiculous."

"Oh, don't be silly."

"And you wondered why you ever said yes to me."

"Come on, Roger, let's order something. I'm hungry."

"I said you could take it back, right? It's not too late, right?"

"Roger, why are you talking this way? What's the matter with you tonight?" she said, putting the menu down to regard him. "Did you have a bad day?"

Roger drew himself up. "I've thought it over, Marjori. You're not going to push me around. That's what our marriage would be like. You pushing me around."

"What?" she said. "Are you crazy or something?"

"Yeah, I must be crazy to think this would ever work. Roger and Marjori. George is right. Even the names don't go together."

"Roger, I'm sorry if I said something."

"And I want the ring back," he said, looking down at her finger. It was a big diamond, not the best, but plenty big.

There was a pause. "Now you *are* being stupid ridiculous," she said pulling her hand away.

"That does it," Roger said standing up. "We're finished. Through. Keep the damn ring. It's a piece of junk anyway."

He left her sitting there speechless for once. He

just walked out, leaving her with the check. Serves
her right, he reflected. He strode down the street like
a man who just beat a bum rap, half exalted, half still
mad. "You can't let them walk all over you," he said
right out loud in the night air. "No sir."

Then he realized he was hungry. He hadn't had
anything since lunch. He stopped in front of a Jew-
ish deli and peered through the steamed-up window. He could see people inside hunched over their
plates. He'd eaten there once before, years ago.
There was a little room in the back too. They fed you
good here, he remembered. So he went in and took a
seat in the back room. It was just as he expected:
warm and cozy, the smell of good meals. An old
waiter shuffled up and took his order, someone who
looked like he'd been putting loaded plates down in
front of hungry customers for forty, fifty years.
Roger ordered corned beef and cabbage, but with
mashed potatoes. And a beer.

The old waiter brought the beer right away and
Roger sat back to enjoy himself. He had done a good
thing. She was not right for him. You can't let them
walk all over you like that. He was feeling good
about what he had done, like a man who just received a suspended sentence and couldn't believe his
good fortune. The ring wasn't worth anything anyway. Then the waiter brought the food. It looked
good and hot, really big portions, but there was
something not right. The plate had a boiled potato.
He looked up at the waiter. "I ordered mashed," he
said pointing to his plate.

The waiter gave him a funny look that said he

couldn't be serious: corned beef and cabbage take a boiled potato. The odd tilt of the old waiter's head said it all: mashed was ridiculous.

"I didn't want boiled," Roger said sitting up in his chair. "I ordered mashed." He was not going to let this guy walk over him. "I want mashed," he repeated.

The old waiter shrugged, picked up the fork by Roger's plate and squashed it through the potato. "OK, here's mashed," he said moving off to take another order.

Later Roger called George. "You a free man?" George asked.

"I let her keep the ring," Roger said.

"You still going with her?" George asked incredulous. There was a pause.

"I don't know, George," Roger said finally. "I'm thinking about it. I haven't made up my mind yet." Then after another pause he said, "You know, George, she costs me, no doubt about it, but the way I see it money ain't everything. I don't have to marry her, you know. And eating alone all the time, hey man, that's for the birds."

THE EDGE OF THE COFFIN

UNLIKE WITH OTHER MEN, nothing ever seemed to bother Peter O. No one ever heard him complain about anything, not ever, not even a backache, or the ever-rising property taxes in the modest enclave of split-levels where he and his wife lived. He was phenomenal that way. He was also, let's be honest here, a horrible bore.

Now the remarkable thing about Rosey, his wife of five years, was that she herself seldom complained, until the events of this story at any rate. She was what you would have to call long-suffering. But you could see little things bothered her all right, like when the backyard fence needed fixing and Peter just smiled and brushed it aside. "Honey, it's really nothing," he'd say. The really nothing was a loose picket that could let some animal in, like a raccoon or the new neighbor's big black dog, which is why Rosey fixed it herself one day when Peter was at work. That didn't bother Peter either, not in the least. Nothing ever did. The truth is he probably never noticed it one way or the other, broken or fixed.

"What do you want for your birthday," Rosey asked him one day.

"Nothing really," Peter said. It was one of his favorite expressions.

"I could get you a Nordic machine, you know, one like Joey's." Joey was the energetic neighbor across the street. Rosey often watched him cutting grass and tending to his property. She would stand sort of transfixed watching through the living room window.

"What would I do with it?" Peter said. It was Sunday and his head was in the financial section. "The NASDAQ finished the week right where it started," he said, without any sign of whether this was a good thing or a bad thing.

"You could stand to lose a little, hon," Rosey said. "Round the middle."

Peter looked over the paper at her. "The Big Board slipped again," he said. He was smiling. Peter liked to register facts like that, keep track of things, things that mattered little to him one way or the other. He tracked the price of coffee futures, no matter that he never so much as dipped a toe in commodities. But none of these facts, good or bad, propitious or unpropitious, ever seemed to bother him. It was just in keeping with his job at the company, keeping track of cash flow.

"The company gave out sixty notices today," he told Rosey when he got home from work on Friday.

"Oh, that's terrible," Rosey said.

"Yeah, well," was all Peter had to say about it.

"I could get you a nice bicycle," Rosey said, changing the subject to his birthday.

"A bicycle?" Peter said.

"A nice red bike," she said. "Wouldn't that be fun? Like the one Joey picked out for me."

"Would I ever use it?" Peter said.

"We could all go riding," she said. "With Joey and Nan. Wouldn't that be nice?"

"Yeah, well," Peter said.

Peter got a bike for his thirtieth birthday, a red one like Rosey's, only this one had a light titanium frame and cost twice as much. Their neighbor Joey from across the street picked it out. Joey knew all about bikes. This one had twenty gears.

"Is red OK? "Joey asked.

"It doesn't matter," Peter said.

Joey was sitting on one of the most expensive bikes in the shop. "This is the real deal," he said, getting off and handing it over.

"I'll never need all these gears," Peter said.

But Joey said, "You'd be surprised. After a while," he said, "you get a feel for each of them."

So that was it. And every Saturday morning around ten o'clock, Peter and Rosey, Joey and his wife Nan, went out bike riding, all riding red bikes and wearing white helmets with a big red stripe. Joey was the captain out in front, and Peter was the rear guard, lagging behind.

"Hey, Pete," Joey said one Saturday dropping back. "That's a pretty nice bike you got there."

"Yeah, it's pretty nice," Peter said.

"Getting the hang of those gears?" he said.

"I'm not used to this," Peter said pumping away.

"Well, hang in there buddy," Joey said, shooting ahead

After the outing they had a hearty lunch at Joey and Nan's. They began to discuss the new neighbor who moved next door to Peter and Rosey a few weeks before. The neighbor with the big black dog.

"Looks like a decent guy," Joey said.

"He never waves back if you try to be friendly," Peter said matter-of-factly.

"Why should he let his dog run loose like that?" Rosey said. "Isn't there a law?"

"And he parks his pickup in the street," Peter said, adding another detail.

"He wakes me up every morning when he goes to work," Rosey said. "Exactly at 4:43. He races the engine and plays the radio loud as anything. It doesn't bother Peter, but I can't get back to sleep."

"Bummer," Joey said.

"Don't you hear him?" Rosey said. "Every morning, at 4:43 like a clock."

Joey smiled and shook his head.

"At 4:43 every morning," Rosey went on, "like an alarm clock, playing his car radio loud as anything. By the time he leaves I'm wide awake," she said. "Every morning. And he's got some ugly, horrible, loud rap music station on."

"Really," Joey said. "Hey Pete, you should say something to him."

"Yeah," Peter said. "Maybe he's trying to wake himself up." Peter had to laugh at that one.

"That's not right," Nan said. "Joey," she said, "why don't we go over and say hello. We should, you know. And we could just mention it."

"Good idea," Joey said.

"I can never fall back asleep," Rosey said.

"Bummer," Joey said again.

Nan shook her head. "That's really disgusting," she said.

"And I'm pregnant now," Rosey said.

At this both Joey and Nan jumped up from their chairs. "Hey, that's terrific," they said. "What great news." And there were hugs all around.

"So I need my sleep," Rosey said, blushing.

Joey turned to Peter. "You gotta talk to this guy," he said.

"I told Peter," Rosey said. "Peter never likes to make waves."

"I'm going to talk to him," Peter said. "He's just warming up his engine."

"Peter will sleep through anything," Rosey said.

"I waved to him right after they moved in," Peter said. "He looked at me like I was weird or something."

"He's the one who's weird," Rosey said. "And that big black dog of his."

"Nan and I'll go over," Joey said. "He can't be all bad."

"That would be just wonderful, Joey," Rosey said.

"No problem," Joey said. "Hey, Pete," he said, "I noticed you having trouble with your gear shift. Maybe needs some silicone. I'll look at it for you, OK?"

"OK, sure," Peter said. "When you have some time."

The next morning, Sunday, Rosey saw Joey and Nan getting in their car. "Peter," she said, "look, Joey has a new car. He must have gotten that yesterday afternoon. Funny they didn't tell us."

Peter joined her at the window. "Camry," he said. "Red," he added.

"That's Joey's favorite color," she said. "Wonder where they go every Sunday."

"Yeah," Peter said, "maybe they're religious or something."

"Do you really think so?" Rosey said.

"Yeah," Peter said. "Probably."

"Do you think they're Catholic?" she said.

"I doubt it," Joey said.

Rosey and Peter watched them leave. "Guess we don't know them that well, do we?" Rosey said.

Rosey went into the kitchen and poured them some coffee. "I didn't sleep after five o'clock," she said as they sat facing each other. "It was our neighbor's dog again. He was barking at something for a whole hour."

"I didn't hear him," Peter said. "Must have seen a raccoon."

"You never do," Rosey said a bit too flatly.

Peter looked at his wife but said nothing.

"You know, hon," she said, "I really need my sleep. I'm not feeling that great these days, you know." After a moment, she added, "We really have to do something about this new neighbor situation."

"Yeah, you're right," Peter said. He got up and peered out the kitchen window. "His pickup's been parked out there all weekend," he said.

"I hope Joey talks to him," Rosey said.

"I'm gonna take care of it," Peter said.

"Joey will do it," Rosey said. "I know he will."

"I'll take care of it," Peter said.

"That's OK, hon, I know you don't like to . . . you know, make waves."

"I said I'll take care of it."

"He's such a nice man, Joey," Rosey said. "We're so lucky to have such neighbors. Nan is nice too, don't you think?"

"She's very nice," Peter said.

"There's something about Joey," Rosey said. "Have you ever noticed how he looks at you? He has such soft eyes."

"I'll take care of it, for crying out loud," Peter said.

Rosey took in her husband for the first time that day. "I know you will, hon," she said. She began to laugh. "I haven't heard that expression in years."

It rained the next Saturday so there was no outing but Rosey invited Joey and Nan to come over for brunch anyway. It was obvious the moment they stepped in the door that something was not right. Rosey and Peter congratulated them on the new Camry but it fell flat.

"Is anything wrong?" Rosey asked when they were seated around the table.

"I left our new car out last night," Joey said. "I shouldn't have. There's a huge scratch on the door. I just saw it now as we were coming over. On the driver's side."

63

"Oh, how terrible," Rosey said. "It's brand new."

"Yeah, that's really rough," Peter said. "Could have been some kids around here last night, you think?"

"Maybe," Joey said. "I wish I knew."

There wasn't much to say after that so they ate their lunch in silence. Rosey had fixed crab cakes, one of her specialties.

"This is really delicious," Nan said after a while.

"I saw our new neighbor," Joey said finally.

"I was wondering," Rosey said.

"Well," Joey said, "it didn't go well. I'll say that much. I won't tell you what he said but when I told him about the noise, I got some four letter words. He's quite a guy."

"When did you talk with him," Peter said.

"Day before yesterday," Joey said, "right after work. He was outside with his dog."

"Well," Rosey said, "it sure didn't do any good. That radio's louder than ever. And yesterday morning he played the radio for almost an hour, at full blast. I was going to call the police but Peter wouldn't let me."

"He was fixing a flat," Peter said.

"Serves him right," said Nan.

"I'm sorry you're having all this trouble," Joey said.

"And we're so sorry about the scratch on your brand new Camry," Rosey said. "I hope there's no connection. I mean about your going over and complaining."

Joey shook his head. "I can't believe that," he said. He turned to Peter. "Well, Pete, they say the rain should clear up by morning. Want to go out?" he asked. Just for an hour or so, right after church. Then we can all go somewhere for a big meal."

"I guess so," Peter said. "If Rosey does."

Rosey touched her belly. "I probably could stand the exercise," she said. "I don't know about the big meal though," she said. And they all laughed.

When they left, Rosey stood by the front window and watched Joey and Nan crossing the street. It was just drizzling by now. She watched them stop by their new red car parked in front of their house and study it, on the driver's side. She saw Joey shake his head and put his arm around Nan's shoulder and draw her close. Then Joey got into the car, the garage door opened, and Joey put it away. In a moment, the garage door came down and Rosey began to cry.

"They are such nice people," she said over her shoulder to no one in particular. "They seem so happy together."

Peter was in the kitchen. Rosey could hear him rattling the dishes. "Hon," she called, "would you come here a minute."

"Can we talk?" Rosey said as Peter came in. "Can we just sit here together for a while," she said.

"Yeah, sure," Peter said, sitting down beside her. "It's still raining some," he said, looking out their picture window.

"We haven't done this in so long," she said.

"Done what?" Peter asked.

"You know, just sit here and talk. I'm glad it's raining," she said. "It makes everything seem closer somehow."

They both saw Joey open his garage door and then, a moment later, close it. "Isn't it terrible about that scratch on their new car," Rosey said.

"Yeah," Peter said. "It's not good. That guy's a nut."

"You think he did it? "Rosey said.

"Could be," Peter said.

"How horrible," Rosey said. "That's really awful."

"Yeah, well," Peter said.

"You really think it was him?" Rosey said.

"I wouldn't put it past him," Peter said.

"What can we do?" Rosey said.

Peter sat there and said nothing.

"The radio's louder now too," Rosey said. "Since that happened. That man's as mean as his dog."

Peter looked out the window. The rain had stopped.

"Joey will figure out something," Rosey said. "He always does," she said, "he always does."

Rosey glanced at Peter and saw that he was looking at her differently. "Are we going to be OK?" Rosey asked suddenly. "You and me, I mean," she said.

Peter gave her a funny smile and said nothing.

Rosey reached for his hand. "I hope our baby will bring sunshine into this house," she said. "It must be the rain. The rain always makes me sad," she said. She squeezed Peter's hand then took hers away.

"Peter," she said, "does it make a difference if it's a boy or a girl?"

"Not really," Peter said.

"That's what I thought," Rosey said. Rosey's eyes

drifted to the window. "I'd like a boy," she said. "We could name him after my father."

"I'd never name him after my father," Peter said.

"Franz Joseph," Rosey said. "That's an emperor's name, you know," she said. "He was head of the Holy Roman Empire."

"Yeah, I know," Peter said. "You've told me that a million times."

Tears welled up in Rosey's eyes. "I'm sorry," she said. "I'm just a silly pregnant woman," she said trying to smile.

Peter tossed his head in a dry laugh. "I should finish the dishes," he said getting up. "That's something I can do at least," he said as he left the room.

"Honey," Rosey called out after him. "I'm sorry," she said.

Rosey looked out the window and saw Joey taking in his empty trash can and she went out to do the same. They exchanged a few words across the street about the weather. Nan came out, saw Rosey and came over to chat.

"Rosey," she said, "is anything wrong?"

"No, I'm all right," Rosey said. "It's all this rain."

"You sure you're all right?" Nan asked with that hesitant look childless women can get when speaking to someone expecting.

"Oh sure," Rosey said. "I just have to get my sleep and I'm fine."

"You must be so happy," Nan said. "We've been trying and trying. But we don't seem able to, Lord knows why. Joey just loves children."

"Joey's so nice," Rosey said. "He's so good."

Nan smiled. "He sure loves his new car," she said.

"Marriage is funny, isn't it," Rosey said. "You never really know what you're going to get."

"It's been the blessing of my life," Nan said. "That's for sure."

"It's so obvious," Rosey said.

Suddenly a noisy pickup drove past them and parked in front of the house next door. The neighbor got out with his big black dog and went into the house.

"Why does he have to park it on the street?" Rosey said. "Every morning I hear him. Like clockwork." Nan shook her head in sympathy.

Then the garage door across the street opened and Joey backed out his new red Camry. "Joey and I have to go somewhere," Nan said. She touched Rosey on the arm. "We'll see you tomorrow," she said over her shoulder as she went to join her husband. "Right after church, OK?"

Joey lowered the window, leaned out and waved. "Tell Peter we're ordering sunshine," he shouted, "and a nice cool breeze. Just for him," he added with a laugh as they pulled away.

As Rosey turned to the house, she saw Peter watching through their living room window.

Matters came to a head in the days that followed. It began early Wednesday morning when a police officer came to the door and asked to speak with them, just as Peter was getting ready to leave for work. Rosey invited the policeman in and called

Peter. The three of them sat down in the living room.

"What's wrong?" Peter said.

The police officer took out his notebook. "I assume you know what happened here this morning."

"We don't know anything," Peter said. "What's going on?"

"Well," the officer said, "there's been some kind of fracas between two of your neighbors, your neighbor across the street and the guy next door to you. He and his black dog. As a matter of fact," the officer went on, "your neighbor across the street is in the hospital."

"Joey!" Rosey cried.

"I guess you know that black dog is pretty nasty," the officer said.

"What's happened?" Peter said.

"Would you please tell us," Rosey said. She was on the edge of her seat.

"Your neighbor across from you was attacked by this guy's dog," the officer said. "The dog bit him pretty bad in the hand."

"Oh, how terrible!" Rosey cried. "How horrible!"

"He's all right M'am," the officer said. "But I believe they're going to have to operate. Looks like a tendon got severed."

Rosey began sobbing softly. Peter placed his hand over his wife's. "How'd that happen?" he said.

"We're trying to piece that together now," the officer said. 'Did either of you see or hear anything this morning?"

Rosey shook her head. "No," she said. "Usually I'm awake, but this morning I didn't hear a thing."

"Well, there's been a lot of complaints about your next door neighbor," the officer said. "About the noise, and especially about this black dog of his."

"I'll bet everybody's been complaining," Peter said.

"Yeah, well somebody got to him real good," the officer said.

"He had it coming," Peter said.

The officer looked at Peter. "You know anything about this?"

"About what?" Peter said.

"The flat tires," the officer said.

Peter hesitated. "The guy had a flat last week," he said.

The policeman shook his head. "I'm talking about what happened this morning. All the tires on his pickup were flat. All four of them."

Peter smiled. "Serves him right," he said.

"Is Joey going to be all right?" Rosey said.

"He'll be all right, m'am. They're testing the dog for rabies but the vet didn't think so."

"How horrible," Rosey said.

"How did Joey get involved?" Peter asked, still holding Rosey's hand.

"That's what we're trying to find out. They tell very different stories, these two. I was hoping maybe you saw something and could help us out."

"I wish we could," Peter said.

"Well somebody in this neighborhood had it in for this guy. The man with the dog thinks it's your neighbor across the street. He says it's not the first time somebody did that to his tires."

"Our neighbor across the street didn't do anything like that," Peter said.

"He couldn't," Rosey said, holding onto Peter's hand.

"I happen to know Joey from church," the officer said. "I don't think he did it either. He's not the type. But, hey, two wrongs were done. It would help to have witnesses so we could sort this out."

"How did Joey get mixed up in this anyway? "Peter said.

"He says he saw the guy this morning standing by his pickup when he was leaving for work, the officer said. He saw he had all those flats. Every tire was flat. He says he went over to see if he could help. That's when the dog attacked him. Joey says the guy sicced the dog on him."

Rosey began to moan softly and Peter drew her close to him. "He'll be OK, hon," Peter said. "We'll go over and see him. You don't die from a dog bite."

The officer put his notebook away and stood up. "Look, this is a nice neighborhood. Never any trouble. Whoever did that to this guy's tires probably did everyone a good turn. If the pickup guy knew who it was, yeah, he could press charges. But I don't think anyone's going to 'fess up, and we're not going to pursue it, that's for sure."

He looked at Peter. "Whoever it was used nails," he said.

"Roof nails," Peter said.

"If you say so," the officer said with sudden new interest.

71

Peter blushed. "At least that was what caused the flat a week ago," Peter said.

"Right, the officer said, looking at Peter. "I'll make a note of that," he said with a broad smile. "By the way," he said as moved to go. "The guy's leaving, so you can all relax. He won't be causing any more trouble. We'll be patrolling this street real good 'til he's out of here."

"He's really leaving?" Rosey asked.

"He was only renting anyway," Peter said.

"Yep, that's my understanding," the officer said to Rosey. "Ask your neighbor, Joey. He knows the story behind that."

After the police officer left, Rosey ran into Peter's arms and cried, "Peter, he's leaving, he's leaving. I can't believe it. It's going to be over."

Peter gave his wife a real hug and said, "Yeah, it's done with now." Then he said they should go see Joey right away.

On the way to the hospital, Rosey kept saying, "I'm so happy, I'm just so happy." She kept reaching for Peter who had to tell her to take it easy or they'd have an accident.

Joey was in the emergency clinic in a little cubicle. Nan was with him and they both brightened instantly when Peter and Rosey poked their heads through the curtain. Peter and Rosey tried to make a fuss but Joey waved it off. He said they were waiting for the surgeon who was going to do the operation.

"He's a member of our church," Nan said.

"No big deal," Joey said.

"It's your right hand," Peter said. "That's tough."

"Yeah, a real bummer," Joey said, holding up his bandages. "You know, I was just trying to help the guy out," he said with a chuckle. "Can you imagine."

"They're going to shoot the dog," Nan said. "There've been lots of complaints about that dog. So it wasn't just us."

"The man is leaving," Rosey said. "A police officer was at our house this morning. He said the man is leaving."

"Yes," Nan said. "Isn't that something? Joey could have pressed charges, you know, but he said he wouldn't, not if the man would leave our street."

"He was just renting," Peter said.

"I think the police gave him some encouragement," Nan said with a laugh. "We heard he has a record."

"Anyway, all's well that ends well," Joey said. Then he began to laugh. "Four flat tires," he said. "That'd drive any guy berserk."

They laughed and talked as if nothing had ever happened. Joey said they'd be back out on the road in a few weeks. "Funny though," he said, "right now Nan's bike is all apart down in our basement. Annual maintenance stuff." He held up his bandaged hand to Peter, "Maybe you can help me out?"

"I'll come over," Peter said.

"I could use a good right hand," Joey said with a laugh. "I could show you a few things, too," he added with a wink.

Peter and Rosey were getting ready to leave when Peter hesitated, came up closer to Joey and said, dropping his voice, "I have to make a confession."

Joey smiled and waved him off. "I think I know what you are going to say," he said out loud. "So say no more. I've done some dumb things in my life too."

Peter laughed. "You know, Joey, he said, I never thought that crud would blame a nice guy like you for those tires."

Joey laughed too. Nan looked a little puzzled. And Rosey, well, she looked at Peter with a face that was positively radiant.

As predicted, several weeks later they were out again bicycling on Saturday morning under weather conditions that could not have been more perfect. Peter this time was wearing a green helmet, something Rosey got for him when he admitted he really preferred green. They bicycled in single file for a few miles with Joey at the head and Peter, as usual, taking up the rear. Then Peter, who knew nothing about road etiquette, on sudden impulse sped to the head of the line and took Joey's place.

"Hey, Nails," Joey shouted after him, "Somebody's found a gear he didn't know he had." And down the line they had a good laugh at this frisky sign of life in Peter O., of all people.

A DIFFERENT KIND OF DAY

IT IS LATE SUNDAY MORNING. The wife, still lovely but with traces of thirty-something wear and tear starting to show, sits at the kitchen table over a cup of coffee. She is studying the kitchen walls. Why did we ever pick such a yellow? she asks herself, grimacing at the wall paper the paperhanger put up only last week. She hears her husband's not-so-steady footsteps coming down the stairs and goes to the stove and pours out a cup of their strong, black Columbian, Sunday-morning fix. She was on the third cup herself.

They had been at a late-evening party the night before. There had been no goodnights. She had been up for hours, fussing with the house. Their eleven-year old, Josh, had gotten up even earlier, miracle of miracles, and left an unholy mess in the kitchen, to say nothing of the living room from whatever he was up to baby-sitting himself last night.

The husband comes in and goes straight for the coffee pot.

"No coffee," he says, shaking the pot.

"Open up those slits, my sweet," she says gesturing to the table.

"All is forgiven," he says sitting down. A prolonged sigh. "Some night," he says, reaching for the Sunday paper.

"Careful it's very hot," she says. "Does someone have a hangover?"

"No, I'm fine," he says, bending over the front page.

"Remarkable," she says to no one in particular.

"I didn't drink that much," he says.

He opens to the sports section. Her eyes wander over the room then come back to rest on the man she gave her life to. He hasn't looked at her yet.

She watches how he feels for the cup and takes it to his lips without skipping a word of print. Maybe he doesn't have a big head but she has a corker.

"I see where they finally got the kid out," she says, pointing to the paper.

"What?" he says.

"You know," she says, "the kid in Texas, the one who fell into the abandoned mineshaft. Glenda told us about it last night, don't you remember? Right near her hometown. They got him out this morning."

The husband rattles the newspaper and turns the page. "The Red Sox lost again last night," he says. "God help us."

"He was in there for thirty-six hours," she says.

She looks for something in the husband's face but the face is fixed on what didn't happen yesterday in some ballpark. Does he ever hear her anymore?

"He was Josh's age, you know," she says.

As if on cue, their eleven-year old rumbles into the kitchen in his many-splendored Nikes, otherwise pure grunge, tossing off an aimless *hi* as he makes for the backdoor.

"Where are you going?" the father says, looking up.

"Out," the boy says.

"I know you're going out," the father says. "I want to know where."

"Over to Jimmy's," the boy says.

"Put your jacket on," the mother says. "That sweater's not warm enough."

"Aw, mom," the boy says. "I'll be hot."

"Do as she says," the father commands.

The boy tears off his sweater and bangs open the hall closet for his jacket.

"What time will you be back?" his mother calls out after him, hearing the front door open. The door slams without an answer.

The father looks at the mother as if somehow it were all her fault, and the mother returns a little smirk that says he's your son, too, you know. That was how the day started. A typical Sunday.

"The boy was hypothermic but he's going to be OK," she says.

"Good," the husband says, buried by now in his own Sunday mineshaft.

They have a whole day ahead of them like this.

"Do you like what I did with my hair," the wife asked, smoothing down her tresses.

The husband looks over at her. "You did something different," he says.

"Do you like it?" she asks.

"Yeah, I guess so," he says. "It's shorter or something."

"You ought to like it," she says. "It's just like Glenda's."

"What's that supposed to mean," the husband says, half putting the paper down.

"I thought her cut looks very smart," she says. "Don't you?" After a pause, she adds, "Their place is so....everything is so....so well appointed. Don't you think so?"

"Yeah, she's got something all right," he says, back into the paper. "I think they call it taste," he says half laughing.

"I know you like her," she says.

"Oh, sure," he says, turning a page. "I'm just crazy about her."

"You always seem to find each other," she says.

"Fellow lawyers will talk," he says, his head shaking in disbelief at the wife, or then again maybe at something he is reading.

"You hardly spoke to the others last night," she says. "I thought it was rude."

"Look, hon," he says, peering over the paper, "she was telling me about the Grover case. She's been given the lead, handling it virtually all on her own. That's a hot child abuse case, you know."

"You didn't see me once all night," she said.

"I saw you talking there with Larry," he says. "You two were laughing it up."

"I have to talk with someone," she says. "I'll bet you don't even remember what I wore," she adds.

"That's a lot of crap," the husband says, tossing the sports section down. "You wore the dress I got you last year for your birthday, and it looked great on you," he says. He rummages for the financial section.

"And you've lost some weight," he adds looking up with the first smile of the day. "I can go for that." The unwanted sections by now are spread out all over the table, half covering the plates, the Danishes, the jams.

"Aren't you going to eat anything?" she asks, clearing the papers away from the pastry with a movement he would have to notice.

"The market had a terrible week," he explains.

"My sympathies," she said. "What goes up must come down. Isn't that the law," she says.

"It's your money too," he says.

A long pause. "I can make more coffee," she says. He says no with his face.

"Anyway, eat something," she says. "Dinner will probably be late, with my head."

He looks at the Danishes, the breakfast rolls, the cheese. "There was a scone in the fridge," he says.

"Josh ate it this morning," she says.

"Josh," he repeats.

Her eyes begin again to roam about the room, resting first on this, then on that. "I've been thinking of having the floor redone with hardwood," she says. "Like Glenda's. Didn't you like their kitchen?" she asks.

Her husband looks up at her, frowning. "You realize this market has hurt us," he says.

"Oh," she smirks and then, in imitation Texas drawl, goes on to say, "Ah recon as how you'all raht theah, counselah. We ah'll just bettah taible thaht theah motion."

"You got it," he says.

Then another big hole in time with nothing between them.

After a while she says, "Do you think she and Hank are breaking up?"

"What in hell makes you think that?" he asks, putting the paper down.

"Just some little things," she says.

"Like what?" he asks. After a pause she says, "I saw the way she hangs on to you, like when you kissed her goodnight."

"You weren't exactly cool with Hank if you ask me," he says.

"He kissed me," she says.

"Hon," he laughs, "that's the way it works. Men are from Mars, right?"

"Do you think they're breaking up?" she asks again.

"No, I don't think they're breaking up," he says. "As a matter of fact, Glenda said they're trying to have another kid."

"She actually told you that?" the wife asks.

"Look, hon," he says, "we're all good friends."

"Yes, I suppose we are," she says. "I suppose we are, in a hazy sort of way."

Before anything more could be said one way or the other, a police siren pierces what was left of the peace that Sunday morning. It came to a stop just down the street from them.

"What in the world?" the husband says, jumping up to the window. "There's a police car stopping at the Anderson's," he says, turning to his wife. Then a second siren enters their cul-de-sac. An ambulance pulls up to the Anderson house just visible from the window.

"There's Jimmy," the wife points, by now at her husband's side. "I don't see Josh," she exclaims. "Where is Josh?" she cries.

The husband is already out the door. "You stay here," he shouts, running down the driveway.

The wife stands frozen for a moment at the window, then goes to the front closet for her husband's jacket and goes out after him.

"What's happened?" the father cries running up to the cop holding the Anderson front door for the EMT's.

"Do you live here?" the cop asks.

"My son is in there," the father says attempting to pass.

"Here, let these guys through," the cop says, drawing him aside for the medics. Suddenly Jimmy's face is at the door.

"Jimmy, where's Josh," the father cries. "What happened?"

"My grandpa fell," Jimmy says, his eyes wild.

"Where's Josh?" the father says.

"He's with grandpa," Jimmy says.

The wife comes up and hands her husband his jacket. "Jimmy, where's Josh?" she says.

81

"He's all right," the husband says. "Stay here, hon, I'll go see what's up. The old grandpa fell or something."

An EMT comes back out the door. "He's dead," he says to the cop.

"What happened?" the wife says.

The EMT looks at her. "Looks like he fell down the stairs," he says.

Josh and his father appear at the door. "Josh is fine," the father says, putting his arm around his boy. The wife looks Josh over then says to the other boy, "Where are your folks, Jimmy?"

"They went to church," Jimmy says, his eyes still rolling in his head.

"Hon," the husband says, "you and Josh go home. I'll stick around here 'til the Anderson's come back."

"I can stay," Josh pleads.

His father sees that Josh is calm, his eyes nice and steady. The father turns to the cop. "Have you been able to notify the Anderson's yet?" he asks.

The cop explains they sent a squad car over to the church. They step aside for EMT's carrying in a gurney.

"How did it happen, Jimmy?" the father says.

Jimmy has trouble with the words. "He fell," he says.

The mother who is still there asks, "Were you with him when it happened, Josh?" Josh shakes his head. More traffic at the door.

"Look, hon," the husband says, "why don't you just go home. You don't have a coat on. Josh and I will stay 'til the Anderson's get here."

The wife hears her husband and son Josh come in the front way and hang up their jackets. "Is everything all right?" she asks as they file into the kitchen.

"He fell down the stairs," the husband says. "Josh heard the fall and ran to help. Jimmy kind of panicked I guess. Josh told him to call 911," the father said, poking his son proudly in the chest.

Josh throws up his fists and beams back. "Dad," he says, "they got there like in five minutes."

"That was wonderful, Josh," the mother says.

"Josh said Jimmy's grandpa died while he was holding him," the husband went on.

"Jimmy?" the mother asks.

"No, Josh was right there with him on the stairs," the husband says, taking in his son.

"How awful," the mother says. "I mean, that was awfully nice you tried to help him, Josh," she says.

"I was like holding his head," Josh says. "It was crooked and it looked like he was trying to say something and then this white stuff came out of his mouth." Josh makes a face.

"Let's not talk about it now," the husband says.

The table had been cleared and places set. "I heated up the Chinese leftovers," the wife and mother says. "You must both be starved."

She says to her husband. "I know you don't usually want a second cup of coffee, but I made fresh."

"Sounds good to me," he says.

They eat and talked about the Anderson's, how they go to church every Sunday but for some reason leave Jimmy home alone with the grandfather. How brave Josh was. How horrible for him to have to see something like this, so close like that, at his age. The old man was bed-ridden. One wonders why he got up, what was he after going downstairs? The Anderson's didn't seem terribly upset, but they strike you as the stoic type. Never had much contact with them except for Jimmy. Jimmy is a nice boy, but not like our Josh. Then the talk dribbled off. A long, comforting, peace-filled silence.

"Do you like the yellow wall paper?" the wife asks after a while, looking around the kitchen.

"Yeah, sure, it's fine," the husband says. "Why, don't you?" he asks.

"Do you think the yellow is too much?" she asks.

"It looks OK to me," he says. "Why, don't you like it?"

"Do you think we made a mistake?" she asks.

"Hey, it looks good," he says. "They did a nice job."

The wife reflects for a while, slowly taking in the room. Finally she says, "I was wondering about it, hon, but you know, I think you're absolutely right." Then she paused and added in her own, soft voice, "You know, counselor, far as I'm concerned, I say the case is closed."

And so begins a different kind of day.

WITH ALL HIS HEART

HE LOVED HER WITH ALL HIS HEART, he said. He said it more and more often in the days leading up to their wedding but the sentiment had a way of striking her like a spring drizzle, as so much pitter patter. Ruby knew her man. She had already sensed the great vacuities in him, the huge interior caverns with nothing much going on in them, nothing much as far as she could tell. He was not the sort a girl dreamt about as she grew and ripened, that nameless presence waiting in the shadows to reach out and say her name and then hold her with such tenderness, so gently, with arms that were strong and confident. Ruby's man wasn't any of that. He was clumsy, even when he tried to take her hand in some special gesture, or when he leaned over to whisper something sweet and intimate. Apart from everything else he was overweight and got loud when he drank. And he was balding. But he had a passable job in a passable company. He liked going places and eating well and laughed at her jokes. He didn't have a clue about dress but had proved himself pliable enough. It might just work out.

Perhaps she could fill these cavities over time. Maybe get him involved in local politics, the way she had been before they started dating. True enough, Ruby could have done better, in an ideal world. No doubt about that. She wasn't anything overweight herself. And she wasn't bad-looking. She was a little tall for a girl, two inches taller than he was, and she liked to wear her spikes, which only made it worse. But he didn't seem to mind. The spikes did things for her back and her legs, which she knew were shapely, really shapely. People noticed her.

She should have been able to do better, but this was what the world was offering to a woman at thirty-five. She had had other chances but she knew she had a sharp tongue. She could take it or leave it but there wasn't any line forming behind him. She decided to take it. It was too late for dreaming. When he told her he loved her with all his heart, she would say I love you too and let it go at that. His name was Roger. Ruby and Roger. Roger and Ruby. Either way it didn't sing exactly but with effort it could work.

They had not been married more than a week when it became clear it would take a lot of work. They had settled into their new place, a cramped little apartment on the Upper West Side. The furnishings were carry-overs from their separate pasts, the queen bed and TV and the chairs from hers, the sofa and the kitchen table from his, and so it went. None of it matched but there wasn't money yet to do much about it. Not yet, but with two of them employed that would eventually change. The problem right now was the people above them. Every night the people above them moved around like foraging elephants.

"What are they doing up there?" Ruby asked.

"They mustn't have a rug," Roger said.

So at this point every evening, after the business of supper had been gotten through with, they turned on the TV and sank into the sofa to complain. Just Ruby complained actually. Roger tried to be more positive.

"I love you with all my heart," he'd say, taking her hand.

"Do you want to go to bed?" she'd say with a hopeless glance up at the ceiling. Anything would be better than this, she'd say to herself.

So they would make love and afterwards he would have a beer and something more to eat and Ruby would get lost in a political magazine. Then she would do her nails and before long it was time to call it a day and go to bed for the night. Usually around this time the people upstairs did the same thing. With the lights out and with silence descending at last, each of them on separate sides of the queen bed, back to back, at home now in unsharable thoughts, slipping one by one into what was becoming, for Ruby at least, the most welcome part of the day, a good night's sleep.

At this rate, Ruby realized, the marriage wasn't going to last. The problem wasn't Roger. It was her. She had always gotten involved in politics, in local election campaigns, for councilmen, or the district attorney, and once even for the mayor. She loved the excitement but she had lost touch with the old crowd when Roger came into her life. The two didn't mix. The marriage had its suffocating side and there wasn't money or opportunity to do anything about it. Roger knew things weren't going too well and did everything he could to make it work. He suggested they go to political meetings together, and they did once or twice but it wasn't the same for her with Roger in tow. Anyway this neat guy, Tony, who she'd worked with and was hoping to bump into, was never there.

Roger took up cooking. He got home from work half an hour earlier than she did and would have the meal cooking away on the stove by the time she came through the door. One night he prepared cabbage with finely chopped apples, the way his mother used to make it. And boiled potatoes. When Ruby said she hated cabbage, Roger reached over and scraped the cabbage from her plate onto his own.

"How can you eat that stuff?" she asked him watching him put it away.

"I grew up with it," he said.

"Gross," she said.

Gradually, Roger learned Ruby's likes and dislikes and catered to them. Ruby always watched her weight and sitting down to a meal meant a sacrifice for them both. Her idea of supper was miniature vegetables, preferably organic, sprinkled with herbs and butterbuds, and some rice pilaf or an arrowroot concoction she'd get at the health food store. Sometimes she allowed herself a piece of free-range turkey breast. There was no question of meat and potatoes and gravy, the food Roger grew up on. Roger began drinking wine instead of beer, and on his own began to add flowers and candles to the table. In the candle light, the place settings and glitter of wine glass lent a touch of romance to their dingy kitchen. Roger lost weight and his color improved and Ruby began to feel better about her husband. She would come through the door at night and find him stir-frying something at the stove, wine glasses filled, candles lit, the kitchen warm and cozy. From time to time there was a surprise by her plate too, maybe outlandish earrings he'd seen in a window (the more outlandish the better as far as she was concerned), or a book about some political figure she had shown interest in. Ruby had only to mention an interest and Roger would have something by her plate the next evening. One night they saw a travelogue about Cancun on TV and Ruby said she always wanted to go there. The next evening there was a book all about Cancun by her plate. It was what they could afford. After a while, when Ruby came through the door her eyes would light up at the scene, especially if something was there by her place at the table. On such nights the tender time they spent after the evening news lingered longer.

But all that only lasted for a while. The people up-stairs were as bumptious as ever. The money wasn't there to do the things they read about in the mags. And the stuff Roger left by her plate was just junk really, and it all began to wear off. It was Roger's mother who saved the day, not with cabbage and finely chopped apples, but by dying and leaving her only son a small amount of money.

"How much did she leave?" Ruby asked with a bright smile when Roger announced the news.

"Enough," Roger said. "Enough for now." Roger loved his mother and didn't feel like smiling.

"Well, was it a lot?" Ruby asked, still bright and smiley.

"Not a lot," Roger said. "Anyway, now we can find another place. And get some things. A king-size bed. And for sure I'm going to take you to Cancun."

"That would be nice," Ruby said.

Roger and Ruby moved shortly after that. They found a quiet place in a building with an elevator. They replaced their queen bed with a king size. Then, not long after moving into their new place, Ruby went back to politics.

It happened this way. It was during her lunch break. She was just walking along Fifth Avenue when she bumped into Tony, a man she had once thought might be the one for her. He was a political operative, smart, fast-talking, exciting to be with, and he moved in the best circles. Politicos running for office invariably sought him out. Ruby knew he would be good for her, but Tony never gave her the right look. Still, she hung around him and got to rub shoulders with some very important people—all in all, the most thrilling times of her life.

"Tony!" she cried, when she spotted him coming toward her. "I can't believe it!"

"Well, hello there," Tony said. "Let's see, Ruby, isn't it? From the mayor's race. I remember you."

"That was so exciting," Ruby said.

"Not very exciting for losers," Tony said. "But, you're right, it was fun. Fun without frills," he said with a big laugh. "The losing side has empty hands when it comes to payback," he winked. Ruby loved the way Tony could joke about anything.

"Where you headed?" Tony asked, looking her over.

"Just for lunch," she said.

"Good," Tony said. 'that makes lunch for the two of us."

At lunch Ruby asked, "What are you up to these days? Whatever it is it must be interesting."

"I'll say interesting," Tony said. "I'm with Calaverti's team. A great bunch of guys."

Ruby smiled but she had no idea who Calaverti was. "He's running for State Senate," Tony said with a wink. "Got a good chance of clobbering that old fart MacElroy."

"Sounds exciting," Ruby said.

"Yeah, it's a ball. Especially to be with a sure winner for once. MacElroy doesn't have a chance in hell. He's dead meat far as I can tell. What with this investigation hanging over him."

"I can imagine," Ruby said, trying to recall what she had read in the papers.

Tony studied his lunch partner. "You know, sweetheart," he said leaning towards her, "it's still gonna be a fight. They have all the money, you know, real money. We'll need all the help we can get—smart volunteers, good people to man the phones, make coffee, a million things." He looked at her with a wink.

"Know anybody?"

"Like me?" Ruby said laughing.

"Yeah, I was hoping, actually," he said with a broad grin.

"Sure, I'd love it. I don't think my husband will mind."

Tony looked down at her ring. "I'm sorry. I didn't realize . . .", he said, his voice dropping off.

"What's to be sorry," she said, placing her left hand in her lap. "Roger won't mind," she added. "He'll be happy."

"OK, then, good," Tony said, taking her other hand.

That evening at the dinner table with Roger, Ruby found an envelope by her plate with airline tickets and hotel booking for three days in Cancun.

"Roger," Ruby said, "it's so sweet of you. But you shouldn't. We can't afford this."

"We can too afford it," Roger said proudly. "I told you we'd do this. And besides, I got a raise today."

"You got a raise! How wonderful for you," Ruby said. "I'm so proud of you."

"And we have a room facing the ocean," Roger said beaming.

Ruby looked at the tickets. "But it's for the Fourth of July," she said.

"Our anniversary," Roger said with a huge grin.

Ruby studied the tickets. "Oh, Roger," she said, after a while. "Can't we put it off until later?"

"Later? Like when?" Roger said.

"Maybe in late November or December," Ruby said. She pointed to the tickets. "These can be changed, can't they?"

"Sure, for a price. But it will cost a lot more in December," Roger said. He saw that she was unhappy. "What's the matter, hon. Are you worried about work? July 4th is a four-day weekend. It's our anniversary."

"It's not that," Ruby said, reaching for his hand. She explained that she had been asked to help the candidacy of a state senator. It was such an opportunity for her. And the summer months were the most critical. It wouldn't be right to leave.

"I see," Roger said. Then, after a moment he asked, "When does this start?"

"Roger," Ruby said reaching to touch him, "I'll be working with someone I knew before. His name is Tony. He's a very sharp political operator. He knows everybody. Maybe you could get involved too."

"Maybe," Roger said. He studied his wife. "You knew him before?"

"Yes, and I've invited him over for dinner some night, to meet you. I told him you were a good chef."

"OK, swell," Roger said. "What does he like?"

"Italian," she said.

"Italian," Roger repeated. "I'll figure something."

"And Roger, I'm sorry about the Cancun trip. We can go some other time, right?"

"I love you, Ruby," Roger said. "Remember, OK? I love you with all my heart."

"I know you do, sweet," Ruby said.

A week later Tony came for dinner. Roger took the afternoon off and prepared *rollatini di Melanzane.*

He had purchased an Italian cookbook and the picture of the rolled-up eggplant looked pretty interesting. By the time Tony came, the house had a glorious smell of Italian cooking.

"The rollatini is delicious," Ruby said in the middle of the meal. Tony had said nothing.

"Thanks," Roger said. He looked at Tony. "I'm not Italian, so I don't know if I did it right," he said. "I followed a recipe more or less."

"It could use more garlic," Tony said with a full mouth.

"I didn't use any garlic," Roger said.

"You didn't use any garlic," Tony said, putting his fork down.

"No. I hate garlic," Roger said. "And Ruby does too."

Tony turned to Ruby. "That true?" he said. "I hadn't noticed," he added with a laugh. "You must be long-suffering with me around."

"No, I like garlic, really," she said. "It's Roger mostly. His mother was Irish."

"German-Irish," Roger corrected.

"German-Irish," Tony repeated.

With that Tony turned to Ruby and to politics and there the two stayed for the rest of the meal. After dinner, Ruby said she had to go with Tony to a campaign staff meeting. It was very important and was just for insiders tonight. Roger said he understood. He did the dishes, watched a little TV and went to bed early. He was fast asleep when Ruby got in late.

Ruby began spending more of her evenings at campaign headquarters, often skipping supper. One

94

night, after eating dinner alone, Roger decided to go down himself and be helpful if he could. Maybe he could man a phone or something also. When he got there people were milling around but Ruby was nowhere to be seen. He asked for her and they told him she had gone out to dinner with Tony. They ought to be back soon. Roger waited around and after a while Ruby came in, making straight for the ladies' room, looking like she had had a few drinks. She flushed when she saw Roger.

"What are *you* doing here?" she said. "What a surprise," she laughed. "I didn't think you cared for this kind of thing." Roger noticed her lipstick was smeared.

"Where's Tony?" he asked.

"Tony?" she said. "He's around somewhere. We just stepped out for a bite."

"Button your blouse," he said quietly.

Roger left and went looking for the man who had smeared his wife's lipstick. Ruby hurried behind him.

"Roger," she called. "Don't do anything stupid."

"You should go home now," he said, turning around. "I am your husband. Do as I say."

"What?" she said.

"You heard me," he said facing her. "I want you to go home. Right now!" This last he said so loudly heads turned to look at the two of them.

Roger went off leaving his wife behind dumbfounded. He found Tony in a conference room with the candidate and some others. Roger barged in past the guard and stood before Tony.

"Keep your dirty hands off my wife," he shouted. Everyone stood up.

"Get him out of here," Tony shouted. The guard tried to grab Roger but he was able to break free.

"You heard what I said," Roger shouted, pushing Tony.

Tony pushed back and Roget hit him in the eye, luckily only a glancing blow. The guards wrestled Roger to the floor and someone called the police. Ruby came rushing in and tried to help her husband but they held her away.

"We don't need this," Tony said to her with disgust, a handkerchief against his eye. "No way."

Sirens sounded and within minutes the police rushed in with drawn guns. The candidate spoke with them quietly and then left for another room with his team. Roger was taken away in a police car.

Ruby took a cab to the police station but was not allowed to see her husband. In the morning, they told her. She went home. On the TV that night they reported a violent incident involving the candidate. Name of assailant has not been released. Motive is unknown.

In the morning Ruby went to see her husband. He was being arraigned on assault and battery charges. Tony filed the complaint. He had seven witnesses lined up.

They led Ruby into a small room. "It's my fault," Ruby said when Roger came in. "I'm so terribly sorry."

Roger said nothing and just looked at her.

"I'm quitting politics for good," she said.

"You don't have to," Roger said. "Just be my wife."

"I want to," she said, beginning to cry.

They held hands for a few moments. "Honey," she said, "will they keep you long?"

"Who knows? Not forever," he said rolling his eyes.

"We'll get a good lawyer," she said.

"Right," he said.

"And when you come out we'll go to Cancun," she said laughing through wet eyes.

"Right," he said, adding with a grin, "If there's anything left after the lawyer."

"And do you know something," she said. "I never told you this but I really love your cooking. I really do."

"No garlic?" Roger said.

"I hate garlic," she said.

"So do I," he said, and they both had to laugh.

NIGHT OF HOLY INNOCENCE

A CHRISTMAS TALE
REFLECTING MATT 2: 6-18

NO ONE KNEW HOW OLD HE WAS, he was that on in years. Too old to tend sheep now, they said. And it was true. He still went out when the sun was up and the sky was clear. He loved it then, feeling gentle breezes there on the hillside, dreaming among the flocks. But the nights now were much too cold for his bones.

Too old for the night watch, but he had Jacob, his little grandson, only too eager to take his place among the shepherds.

"Our sheep begin to know your voice," the old man said to his grandson just that afternoon. "That's good," he said.

"Grandfather," little Jacob said, "Uncle Ezra is not well. You heard?"

"Yes, I know," the old man replied.

"And father is still away," Jacob went on, "so who will watch the sheep tonight? There's no one."

The old man had to smile. "No one but you?" he said, the smile spreading as he regarded his grandson.

"Is it all right, Grandfather?" the boy said. "I'm not afraid."

The old man nodded. "It will be good for you," he said.

"Oh, thank you Grandfather!" the boy cried as he scampered away.

The sun was just setting as Jacob came by to see his grandfather.

"I'm going to go now," he said. "To relieve Uncle Izzy." Then he said, "Would you give me your blessing?"

The old man smiled and stretched out his hand. "I do bless you, my son." Then he added, "Be watchful, Jacob. They caught some thieves two villages over. And the night is long."

The boy nodded and was about to depart when he stopped. "Grandfather," he said, "do you remember that man who knocked on our door today, looking for a place to stay? He said his lady was going to have her baby."

"Yes, I spoke with him, but we could not help him," the old man said shaking his head. "Your little brother is due any moment now. Your mother sadly could never take in guests, not in her condition."

"Are you sure it's a brother?" Jacob said brightening.

"I'm quite sure," the old man said. "I've had dreams and premonitions. And I know that this little boy will give the Lord Our God glory in some special way."

The boy looked up at his grandfather. "What does it mean to give God glory?" he asked.

The old man smiled again. "Well, son," he said, "we give God glory every time we fulfill his Will, whatever that may be. It can even be that the Lord God will ask for a very great sacrifice." The old man said this with a trace of sadness in his voice.

"So my little brother is going to do something big for God," Jacob said, his eyes large as an owl's.

"I believe so, yes," the grandfather said. "I trust this premonition."

"Grandfather," the boy said. "What is a premonition?"

The old man laughed. "Get along with you," he said. "Uncle Izzy will be wondering where you are."

"And what about me, Grandfather?" the boy said. "Do I give God glory guarding the sheep?"

"Even that," the old man said.

"So bless me, Grandfather," the boy said.

"I already did, son," the grandfather said with a chuckle.

"No, Grandfather, tonight I need a special blessing."

The old man could not help but smile once again at his little grandson. He placed both his hands on the boy's head and prayed, "May the Lord Our God keep you, Jacob, throughout the night, and may He show you his great kindness."

And with that little Jacob ran off to the fields.

Early light was barely visible in the eastern sky when the old man heard his grandson's voice.

"Grandfather! Grandfather!" the boy cried, bursting into his room.

The old man whispered, "Hush, son, you mustn't wake your mother."

"Grandfather," the boy went on, unable to contain himself. "We saw angels in the sky, really! And the most unbelievable baby!"

"What are you saying?" the old man said clearing sleep from his eyes. "Quiet down now. Tell me what happened."

"We were there on the hill," the boy cried unable to calm his excitement, "watching the sheep when suddenly this light lit up the sky, and we heard the most beautiful singing."

"Singing?" the old man questioned.

"Yes, Grandfather. And then we saw angels, the sky was filled with them, all praising God."

The old man, fully awake now, drew the boy down beside him. "Tell me, Jacob," he said, "what did you see?"

"I saw that Lady and her Baby," he cried.

"Where was this, Jacob?" the old man said.

"She was in that abandoned stable in the east cove, just outside the village. The Baby was lying in a manger."

"In a manger?" the old man said.

"Yes, Grandfather," Jacob said. "The Lady was kneeling by the Baby. Her Husband too. She was so very beautiful. But Grandfather, it was this Baby. The angels told us to come and worship Him."

The old man fell silent, studying his grandson. "Tell me," he said softly.

"I can't explain it, Grandfather," the boy went on, more quietly now. "How peaceful it felt to be there. The others held back, but I went right in and the Lady took me and showed me her Child."

"Just you?" the old man said, breaking into a smile.

"All the shepherds were there, Grandfather, only not as close as me. They saw the Baby too, a little boy. The Lady said his name is Yeshua. And, Grandfather, I think the Baby blessed me. "

The old man looked for a long moment at the boy beside him, a dreamy light settling into his eyes. "You have been blessed indeed," he said at length.

"Oh, Grandfather," the boy cried, "how peaceful it was to be in this Baby's presence!"

Just then a woman's piercing wail came from another room. The old man stiffened. "Your mother is entering labor," he said getting up. He turned to Jacob. "Go to Hillela, the midwife," he said. "Have her come at once."

The boy ran off and the old man went outside. He stayed there looking up at the sky. There were no angels. Again he heard a cry of pain within the house, and a deep sadness seeped into his heart. But there was a throb of joy too. He knew those dreams and premonitions were true. He did not understand how it would be, but he knew it was so. These baby boys, the Lady's newborn Child and the child his daughter was about to deliver—both so very inno-cent—yet both he knew were destined to die, each for the sake of the other and for all, and by their sacrifice to give great glory to God.

102

BRIAN'S LAW

A ROMP THROUGH EINSTEIN'S WORLD BY A CHILD PRODIGY WHO THINKS EINSTEIN GOT IT WRONG

Physics is pure objectivity. There's no place for subjectivity in physics.
—*Albert Einstein*

THEY SAY IT ALL BEGAN some 14 billion years ago, give or take. Nobody was there of course, but that's what they say. You have to admit people who can get their mind around something like this, that it was 14 billion years and not 14 trillion years or maybe even a whole lot less, are impressive and have to be few and far between. I know I could never have figured it out, not in a hundred lifetimes. And not only that, they figured out how it all happened too, well almost anyway. First there was nothing, or practically nothing, and then, by some quantum quirk or other, this strange *thing* happens to show up. No warning, no explanation, no nothing. Just this strange something suddenly there, a packet of incredible energy that held all the power you need to run a universe. Just

103

imagine, all the power for the zillions of galaxies, to say nothing of our own sun and our puny earthquakes and hurricanes, all there right from the get go. All this in whatever it was that just came along with no place to go because before it came along, there was no such thing as place. Not even a place for it to happen.

Really strange, though of course whatever happened just then couldn't really have been strange, when you think about it, because who was around to think, *Hmm, that's odd.* Okay, maybe God was around, but he wouldn't have said anything like that. This first something or other could have struck him like an artist might feel when he steps back from his canvas, *Hey, that's really good!,* but hardly strange.

Anyway, to get on with it, these physicists say what happened was that this unforeseeable something just appeared, out of nowhere, the closest thing to nothing that you could get and still be something, the first something ever, and it had so much pent up energy that it started to inflate itself at blinding speed like a huge cosmic balloon. And on top of it, it had to create the vast cosmic space it needed as it went. And they say it hasn't let up, it's still expanding like crazy, and still making room for itself as it rips merrily along in all directions at once.

Truly amazing. So now we have this tiny little spec of whatever inflating itself with a cosmic roar, and all kinds of new things start to show up on stage, a whole mess of unheard of oddballs—quarks and pions and neutrinos and anti-neutrinos and whatever, and then, out of that incredible soup, completely new things like atoms and molecules and eventually, way, way down the pike, even things like tennis balls, and, thank God, our rare, *ex nihilo* physicists. What would we do without them?

I don't know what to marvel at most, actually, that something should have just inexplicably popped up from nowhere, bringing along with itself the somewhere it needed for itself to happen, or what this crazy spec of energy wound up producing, the teeming world we have today and these incredible genius minds. First we have this unheard of "singularity," then quarks, molecules, and eventually ectoplasm that organizes itself into thin folds of grey matter with PhDs that give out theories of everything, explaining it all, lock, stock and barrel, start to finish.

Talk about the tail wagging the dog!

Think about it. From molecular soup to a theory of everything, in real time, while the whole shebang is still blowing up! You wonder if it keeps on going, what unheard of things will happen next? Maybe we will be able to go back in time and take a grandstand seat and watch it happen! I can see it now: some university physics lab with a ticket booth to the greatest show on earth. Not my idea, mind you. Some of these guys really think time is a shuttlecock, not an arrow, so why not double back to the starting line some day. No kidding, we owe these gents a great debt, since it really bothers a guy/gal not to know where she/he came from, or where we're all heading on this crazy cosmic rollercoaster. I'm really serious. Not that any of it is good news exactly. It's all supposed to collapse one day in on itself, time, space, and all the stuff, PhD's included, all buried in some infinitesimal black sink hole with no place to go again. I can see why some guy cried out, *Stop the world, I want to get off.* Must have been one of those brainy astrophysicists who saw the end coming. Or maybe one of those guys who swallowed that line that if you could see out far enough, all you'd be looking at is the back of your own head. So much for visionaries. Like I said, these guys are really something.

Well, that's enough of that. This is supposed to be a story about one of those brainy, latter day developments of the Big Bang, about a little snot by the name of Brian Albert Einstein McCor, a budding boy genius with a mop of hair just like Einstein's, a fourteen-year-old who had everything all figured out by himself. A lot of people took this spunky little brat for some kind of singularity in his own right and would have loved to find a black hole to stuff him in!

No doubt about it, Brian was a prodigy. But obnoxious. "A boy your age should be polite to people," his mother would tell him.

But Brian said he wasn't being rude. "Is it my fault if people don't know what they are talking about?" he would answer.

His mother would pat his hair down at such times and tell him, "Don't ask so many questions. Just be nice. And promise you'll get a haircut."

Brian entered the freshman class at Princeton

right after his fourteenth birthday with an already declared concentration in physics. Not very deep into his freshman year, Brian's mother was asked to drop by and see the head of the physics department, Professor Zelnitsky. He wanted to talk to her about her son.

Brian's mother was hardly surprised. Brian was keeping up the family tradition. Brian after all had been named after her grandfather, Brian Ballister Duncove who for a quarter of a century had been Lambert Professor of Physics at Princeton. This was back in the heydays when the German Einstein and the Austrian Goedel walked the shady streets of this charming Jersey town like two towering giants, talking German and making everyone around them feel like mental midgets. Brian's mother already saw her son one day joining the ranks of Duncove, Einstein, and Goedel. It was inevitable that the physics department at Princeton would quickly recognize in her son the seed of future greatness.

The truth is that Brian's namesake, Brian Ballister Duncove, would already be forgotten in the annals of physics were it not for some unflattering anecdotes. It was said locally that Einstein could never remember Duncove's name, which must say something about the latter's contribution to science. But the real killer was when Einstein once referred to Duncove as Herr Dummkopf. Not that Brian Ballister Duncove was entirely inconsequential. He was one of the last holdouts in the world of physics against Einstein's theories of relativity. What really galled him was Einstein's ravaging of the notion of

time. Imagine thinking that the time of day depend-
ed on whether a person was moving or stationary!
God keeps the time, Duncove once shouted at a meeting. Duncove was an Episcopalian and liked things to
be neat and orderly. It was all rather ironic actually
because Einstein himself had recourse to a similar
defense later when the new generation of physicists,
the quantum kids—Einstein called them Quan-
tumkinder—sought to disconnect effects from their
causes, of all things, claiming that not causality but
chance and probability accounted for what happens
in the universe, from distant quasars right down to
the new leaves appearing each spring on the trees of
Princeton's charming lanes. Einstein, who loved his
walks and bike rides down these lanes, dismissed
such talk with his famous retort, *God doesn't play dice!*

Doubtless young Brian knew all about these controversies and had already formed an opinion as to
where time and dice stood with God and vice versa.
But it is safe to say none of these controversies regis-
tered with Duncove's granddaughter, Brian's mother,
as she approached the offices of the physics chairman
at Princeton College with her genius son in tow.

"Professor Zelnitsky," Brian's mother said, reaching for the professor's hand, "I believe you must have
known my grandfather, Brian Ballister Duncove. He
was . . . "

"Yes," Professor Zelnitsky interrupted, returning
to his desk. "I knew him slightly. Your son I see is
attempting to carry on the family tradition," he said
trying to be pleasant. The professor's effort at a smile
collapsed as he watched the youth move right past

him to the bookshelves that lined his office. What was worse, just then rays of the afternoon sun broke through the office window and fell directly on the kid's unruly Einstein hair. The professor's face made it abundantly clear that the halo effect was quite uncalled for. The mother for her part resolved to remind her son that Einstein accepted haircuts at his age. Brian for his part was busy checking titles.

The professor snapped to the point. "Madame," he said, "let me be frank. One of our instructors feels your boy is not ready for Princeton. He has asked me to remove your son from his class."

Brian's mother sat up abruptly. "Brian's SAT was 1600," she said.

"Yes, well," the professor went on, "let me be more direct. Your boy is fourteen, I believe. Still an adolescent. Perhaps in a few years . . ." he said, his voice trailing off. He could not take his eyes off this unacceptable play of light on the boy's head as he flipped pages in one of his volumes.

"What's age got to do with anything?" Brian shouted out over his shoulder. His voice cracked, the lower registers of his voice still being new to the job.

"Brian," his mother said, "that's not polite. Come over here and sit by me." She patted the seat next to her and then turned to Professor Zelnitsky. "Are you suggesting Brian is having difficulty with his class work," she asked. The arch of her eyebrows suggested this was hardly possible.

"Not exactly, Madame," the Professor said. He looked over at the boy now slouched down beside his mother, still peering into one of his volumes. "This has to do with attitude," he added, "not aptitude, not for the moment at least."

Professor Zelnitsky picked up an examination bluebook on his desk. He explained that Brian's physics instructor had given a little ice-breaker quiz to the freshmen class asking them to demonstrate how a barometer could be used to measure the height of a building. "Not only did Brian not answer the question, the professor said, he . . ."

"I did so answer it!" Brian cried, nose poking up, a trace of red in his boyish blue eyes.

The professor waited for the moment to settle and then opened the bluebook. "Your son wrote one sentence," he said. He began to read aloud, the cost to his dignity telling in every word:

"You can measure the height of a building with a barometer by attaching a string to the barometer, going to the roof of the building, lowering the barometer to the ground, and then measuring the length of the string used."

The professor put the bluebook down. "That's not even clever," he said looking at the mother.

"I answered the question," Brian said, boyish eyes hardening.

"Your son knows very well what he was doing," Zelnitsky said. The poor man looked out his office window and thought about things he could be doing.

A wry smile crept over the boy's face. "There's lots of answers to that question," Brian said catching the professor's reluctant eye. "Like you could go to the architect and offer him the barometer if he would tell you the building's height."

The professor's cold stare forced Brian to quicken the pace.

"OK," he said hurriedly, "on a sunny day you could put the barometer on the ground next to the building and measure the two shadows."

The professor's stare grew ominous and Brian had to turn to his mother. "You figure the ratio of the barometer's shadow to the barometer's height, he said to her. And then, using the ratio, you take the building's shadow and get the height. Using the ratio," Brian repeated to her hopefully. He swung back to the professor. "Or you could . . ." he began, but now it was his turn to be cut off.

"This has nothing to do with physics," the professor said aloud to the mother. "Nothing whatsoever," he repeated. Professor Zelnitsky came out briskly from behind his desk. This had gone far enough.

"I can give you physics," Brian said, throwing the professor's book down, voice now in excitable registers. "Take the barometer with the string attached and go up to the roof. Then lower the barometer so that it almost touches the ground and start swinging it like a pendulum. You can use the period of the arc to calculate the height of the building. Or you could just do something stupid like just dropping it from the roof and timing the fall."

Brian looked at the professor with a mixture of merriment and boyish hope. "32 feet per second squared," he said turning to his mother.

The professor stood before them, sour face, addressing the mother. "I'm sure your boy knows the simple answer to a simple physics question," he said. "That's clearly not our problem."

"What's a correct answer?" Brian said, voice rising. "I answered the question, right? I can give you some more ways to measure the stupid building . . ."

The professor stuck out his hand like a traffic cop. "Young man," he said. "We don't mock science in this department." He looked over at Brian's mother who fell into a fit of blinking. "You understand we are not running a day school here at Princeton," he said. The professor turned to go back to his desk. The matter could now be considered closed, *finito.*

Brian's mother reached for her purse and put on her glasses.

Brain, undeterrable, leapt up after the professor. "I have a question," he said.

The professor stopped and turned slowly in his tracks, an effort not unakin to what it would take to bring the new Queen Mary painstakingly about in Manhattan's East River. "What is it," he managed at length.

"You knew Professor Einstein," Brian asked, "rght?"

Professor Zelnitsky studied the boy for a long moment. "Yes, I knew him," he allowed at length. "Why do you ask?"

"I heard you had long conversations with him," Brian said, eyes lighting up.

Zelnitsky permitted himself a restrained nod. "We spoke a few times," he said. "When I was a student here." The professor sat down tentatively, on the very edge of the chair next to Brian. "I was quite a bit older than fourteen I must say," he added.

"For Einstein," Brian said, "everything in physics begins with the observer, right?"

"That's hardly Einstein," the professor said. "You don't do physics without observation."

"Right," Brian said. "But I mean Einstein went further than that. He makes everything start with the observer. Like if there's no observer, there's no universe."

"You can put it that way," Zelnitsky said, voice dull as wet noodles.

"So," Brian said, "who observed the Big Bang?"

The professor laughed for the first time that morning. "Einstein had nothing to do with the Big Bang," he said. "He never liked the theory, as a matter of fact."

"But there was a Big Bang, right?" Brian said.

Professor Zelnitsky stood up and backed away. "If there was a Big Bang, young man, it was a singularity, which means physics knows nothing about it. Not a thing. Not even Einstein."

Being a self-respecting department chair at an Ivy League school, with scores of publications to his name, Zelnitsky should have ended the session right then and there and, indeed, surely would have were it not for Brian's next remark.

"I think Einstein was wrong," he said. "About the observer, I mean. And he's wrong about some other things too," he added.

Intelligent as Zelnitsky was, this was momentarily too much even for him to absorb—a fourteen year old in his office questioning the last 100 years of science — not before Brian, that is, seizing the moment, began to do a core dump. Such is the way with genius they say. Long silences as if nothing is going on, maybe even fourteen years of it, and then things start pouring out. That's exactly what happened with Einstein, too, over a 100 years ago in 1905, except that at his age then, Einstein was almost old enough to be Brian's father.

"What are you saying?" Zelnitsky asked despite himself.

"Einstein got it wrong," Brian said, sitting up and running fingers through his hair.

"Einstein got it wrong . . ." Zelnitsky repeated incredulously, a short sentence he found impossible to parse.

"Yeah," Brian said. "Einstein's world is upside down. The observer is very important, sure, but the observer arrives last in the sequence of things, not first the way Einstein has it. If A is going to observe some B, B's got to already be in place, right? So A, the observer, can't be so absolutely up front the way Einstein has it. And Einstein's observer is a loner too, isolated from every B by the signals that connect them, and these signals can travel no faster than the speed of light, so no A is ever in sync with any B. Einstein is absolutely against simultaneity. And he's wrong about that. He's wrong about some other things also."

The enormity of the nonsense he was hearing seemed to disorient Zelnitsky. The boy must be mad.

"Yeah, "Brian said, core dump now in full swing.

114

"Take motion, for example. Suppose God went around and zapped everything in the universe except a single atom. According to Einstein, that atom couldn't move. That's because to him, the only way that observer A can say that some B is moving is because he sees B moving relative to himself or to something else, right? So for Einstein there is no such thing as pure motion in empty space. Because the observer can never detect pure motion, only relative motion, motion of some B relative to some A. So if there's no observer around, a solitary atom can't move. That's what you get if you make the observer the one true god."

Zelnitsky remained speechless, stupefied at the desecration taking place before him. Had not the great Einstein himself come into this office in his day, sat in these very chairs? But there was no stopping Brian at this point.

"So how did motion get started in the first place?" Brian went on, waving his arms as if to take in the entire universe. "When the Big Bang went off, if there was only one thing around at the start, some incredible, solitary packet of energy or whatever, then according to Einstein, it would have to be frozen. It couldn't move, not until something else showed up, right? So the original thing could move relative to it. Otherwise it's frozen. And if there were a bunch of things at the start, they couldn't start out moving either, because according to Einstein, they would all have to depend upon the speed of light to put them into a relationship so they could move relative to each other, like Einstein said. So until that light signal came along, there's no motion, all these things are frozen. That's assuming there even was such a thing as photons, you know, back there at the get go. Whatever, the universe didn't start off expanding, it started out frozen solid, right? Until the first light signals got around to everybody and said, OK guys, relationship established, everybody start moving." Brian began to giggle.

Zelnitsky roused himself at this last bit of idiocy. He spoke not a word, just came over and held out an icy hand to the mother and said, "Good day, Madame." Then Zelnitsky went to the door of his office, tore it open, and with a sweeping gesture indicated the room must be vacated, "Now, at once."

Zelnitsky stood in the doorway waiting for deliverance but Brian, ever the brat, remained in his seat looking down at the floor, struck by some new thought. The mother stood by her son, not knowing what to do, torn as it were between an implacable force and an immovable object, to put it in physical terms.

"Good day, Madame," the professor repeated in a preternaturally loud voice that must have raised eyebrows in the neighboring offices. Brian looked up at this point, and with enough good sense to break his chain of thought, he got up and joined his mother. In the doorway, though, he stopped and looked straight into the eyes of the hapless Chair.

"That's where Einstein made his big mistake," he said, "by starting out with a lonely observer who's only connected to the rest of the world by the travel of light. But, "Brian added gleefully, "I think I know how to fix it."

"Good," the professor said refusing the look, "and maybe you can measure the height of your 'stupid building' while you're at it."

Whereupon the door was shut, unmistakably, leaving Zelnitsky in peace at last.

Outside on their way down the mother said, "Brian, why can't you just be nice?" But Brian was worlds away, working something out.

"Nothing is ever really solitary," he mumbled. Then suddenly a look of total glee lit up his face of fourteen years. "*Ein*stein, *Zwei*stein," he cried out, and once again fell into giggling.

"And promise your mother you'll think about getting a haircut," his mother ran on, running a finger through Brian's hairy tangle and shaking her head at what she had brought into the world.

In the elevator, descending with his mother, while the universe was still expanding and the good professor Zelnitsky was recovering his peace, Brian then and there formulated a new first law of physics, even replete with equation. It struck him as so fundamental it would come to be known as an ultimate law, as Brian's Law, a law above all laws. He knew it was more fundamental than $E=mc^2$, but even so, Brian wished like anything he had a chance to talk to old Einstein and find out what the master thought of it. Brian never had a real father to go to, and even if Einstein was wrong, to Brian Einstein was like the father he never had.

Anyway, this is what Brian came up with in all its sudden, disarming simplicity:

117

Nothing exists by itself.

True, his law had none of the arcane majesty of $E=mc^2$, but to Brian's mind his law was infinitely deeper. Just as Einstein had looked beyond Newton's absolutes of space and time and discovered relativity, Brian knew that he had just seen beyond relativity. And what he glimpsed was a truth as absolute as any could be — *nothing exists by itself.* Its simplicity spoke its defense. And the equation that expressed it was as simple as could be:

$$R = M + O.$$

Where:

R stood for *Cosmic Reality*, the everything that exists.

M stood for the *Material* world withut the observer (i.e., R-O).

O stood for the *Observer*.

And here was Brian's explanation, for what it's worth. The way Einstein and modern physics saw it, the R, the Cosmic Reality, is always going to be on uncertain grounds because its main component, M, the material world, can only be said to exist if observer O affirms M. So M can only exist if O says so. And O's observations of M are shaky because O is completely isolated from M by the time delay associated with light travel. True, for Einstein the speed of light is the glue, the one absolute that holds the world together, but it's just as true to say that light travel separates O from M and keeps them both in isolation and uncertainty. Now, for Brian, all this gets reversed with his new law. The observer O comes last, not first, and O has a world to observe because that world, M, is already there to begin with, as a given. The observer O does not have to reach out to find M, this M, the material world, is already there ahead of O, reaching out to him. And M's givenness to O gives R, the cosmic reality, a steady, not a shaky foundation. But most especially, Brian's law holds that the observer, O, is not an island disconnected from the material world, from M, disconnected until M's light signals get around to O. Reality doesn't work that way, Brian says. Reality, R, is *always* M + O. *Nothing exists by itself.*

And then, in the very next breath, Brian realized his law had a serious flaw. The problem was still the observer. True, the observer is a finisher not a starter, and true, the observer is never stuck off by himself. R, the cosmic reality, was always M + O, inseparably. All true. Yet, there was still something about the observer that escaped him, something he needed to figure out. No problem, the boy Brian had no doubt it would fall in place soon enough. Idiocy or not, as you will see, the Einstein kid was just getting started.

So that's the way it was with our boy Brian by the end of his first weeks at Princeton. He was already on his way to redefining not just the science of physics, but, heaven help us, the science of everything. In his own mind, to be sure. As for the outside world, Brian quickly became an eccentric presence on the Princeton campus, what with his Einstein hair and the stories bandied around about him and Zelnitsky. Miraculously, Brian was not removed from Physics 101, probably because he stopped going to class, except on the days exams were given to absolutely cream them. Brian used the hour to sit in on an advanced course in theoretical physics, given for upperclassmen by an elderly member of the faculty, a good buddy of Zelnitsky's. Brian would slip into the back of the lecture hall and slouch down in a chair, every so often mumbling at something the professor would say. The presence of this muttering kid with the hair slouched in the back of the lecture hall amused the upper-class students no end. And luckily the old professor never noticed. He spent most of his time with his back to the class, scrawling equations and diagrams on a blackboard the length of the platform, lecturing over his shoulder.

It happened, however, that one day this professor, in a relaxed moment during a lecture on relativity, set aside his chalk and began to reminisce about an encounter he had with Einstein back in the days when he too was an undergraduate. He related how he and a few other students went over to the nearby Institute for Advanced Studies one afternoon where Einstein worked, i.e., did his heavy thinking, hoping they might get a chance to meet the master. They got into the building on some pretext or other and then all paraded single file past the great man's office. Happily Einstein's door was open and when he saw them he waved them on in. Einstein was in a good mood and gave them coffee and before long began entertaining them with some amusing thought experiments, the sort of mental gymnastics that had made him famous. But the thought experiments that day were hardly serious and mostly poked fun at Einstein himself.

Einstein said there were two rocket ships that took off, one heading in one direction at near the speed of light, the other heading in the opposite direction also at near the speed of light. On the first rocket ship is Herr Doctor Professor Z and on board the second ship, going in the opposite direction, is his wife, Frau Herr Doctor Professor Z. Now, obviously, if each spaceship is going in opposite directions at near the speed of light, then the distance between them is increasing at nearly twice the speed of light. How, Einstein asked, can this be? We know, since relativity, he said, that no event in the universe can take place faster than the speed of light and yet here we have a distance increasing at nearly twice the speed of light.

The professor stopped and smiled at this point. "So," he said, pointing to the class, "how do you answer Einstein here?"

A number of hands shot up and the professor nodded to a bright young female student in the front row. She stood up and explained that Einstein had shifted the scenario from physics to mathematics.

"When we talk about the distance increasing at twice the speed of light," she said, "we are not dealing with a physical fact. No spaceship has actually traversed this distance at nearly twice the speed of light. The distance separating the Doctor and his wife is a mathematical construct, arrived at by summing two physical facts, the speeds of each of the airships.

The problem turns on mathematics, not physics," she said and sat down.

"That is very good," the professor allowed. "You are quite right. Einstein told the story to remind us that physics deals with facts and mathematics deals with, well, with mathematics." Everyone in the class laughed knowingly at this remark.

Then the professor went on. "But there was more to the thought experiment," he said. "The Frau Doctor was having a birthday the next day of their journey, and the Herr Doctor wanted to send her a birthday greeting. Especially because he had missed doing so the year before, at some expense to their marriage. So, 24 hours into the journey, he sends her a message in the form of light signals. Now, Einstein wanted to know, given that these two people are fleeing from each other in opposite directions at near the speed of light, what are the chances that this light signal will ever reach the Frau Herr Doctor in time for her birthday?"

Again, hands shot up and the professor called on a young male student up near the front.

"The signals will never reach her," he said. "The photons of light will barely leave Herr Doctor's spaceship."

"And why is that?" the professor asked.

"We can see this by simple analogy," the student said. "If you are standing on a moving platform going one hundred miles an hour in one direction, and you have a gun with a muzzle velocity of one hundred miles per hour and you fire it in the opposite direction of travel, the two velocities, moving in opposite directions, cancel each other out. The bullet will just drop to the ground. The doctor's spaceship is traveling in one direction at near the speed of light, so the same can be said for any light signal sent back in the opposite direction to the Frau Doctor. It'll go nowhere or at best just crawl away."

The bright young woman in the front row raised her hand again. "That's nonsense," she said. "Once they're sent off, the light signals have their own independent velocity. Besides, we know that travel at velocities approaching the speed of light slows time down dramatically. An equation could probably be worked out where Herr Doctor's message might very well catch up to the wife's spaceship in time for her birthday."

Another hand shot up. "What about the curvature of space?" this student said. "These spaceships can't escape the sun's gravity and the space around the sun is warped by its mass, as Einstein proved, so if you are traveling at near the speed of light with time slowed down, then these two spaceships will soon be traveling towards each other, not away. Hey, the professor could even be waving to his wife on her birthday."

The professor nodded and added with a chuckle, "So long as their trajectories are in the same plane and not worlds apart."

The class found all this amusing and the professor concurred with a comical gesture. "We had fun with Einstein that day too," he said. "Einstein told us we can be thankful God does not ask us to move about at the speed of light, so we don't have to worry about such problems. Then Einstein indicated we should leave because he had work to do. But before we left he told us one more thing. With a knowing twinkle in his eye, he said, 'So you young people remember now, when you get married, if we want to keep peace in the family, we should not put too much distance between ourselves and our spouses.'"

The professor laughed, thinking of Einstein's own marital problems, "I guess he would know."

The class enjoyed all this very much and the professor, pleased with the effect, looked at his watch just as Brian strolled up to the front.

"I have a thought experiment," he announced.

The professor had heard about this kid with the hair from Zelnitsky, but before he could react Brian began to speak. He had a thought experiment he wished to present, he said, something that occurred to him during the previous discussion. He explained that it concerns an event that takes place on the first spaceship and that affects the second spaceship simultaneously, independently of the speed of light.

Brian, not bothering with permission, turned to the class and began, his voice strong and no longer cracking. "It happens," he said, "that Herr Doctor on the first spaceship gets sick and dies. His death affects the Frau Doctor on the other spaceship at that very moment because now it makes her a widow. So here we have an event on the second spaceship which is effected *instantaneously* by an event on the first spaceship. The two events are simultaneous.

According to Einstein, that can't happen. For Einstein, there is no such thing as simultaneity. No event on the first spaceship can affect the second spaceship at a rate faster than the speed of light travel. And yet here we have two interlocked events which occur instantaneously and simultaneously, at great distances from each other, having nothing to do with the limits imposed by the travel of light. How does Einstein explain this?" Brian turned back to the professor, eyes bright with innocent hope.

The professor, caught between annoyance and amusement at such a silly notion, tilted to the silly notion first, encouraged no doubt by the growing titters in the hall.

"Well," he asked, "what is the event on the second spaceship? The wife doesn't know she is a widow. And until she knows, there is no second event."

"She doesn't have to know it," Brian says. "What's true for the Doctor is true for the wife."

"Yes, that's true of course, but true in the order of logic," the professor said. "There are no physical effects as yet. No effects until she learns that she is a widow."

"It's not just logic," Brian insisted. "There are physical effects also."

"And how is that?" the professor said, beginning to enjoy the class reaction. "The poor lady," he said, "is still going to be angry that her husband missed her birthday." The amusement in the hall increased and the professor grew more pleased with himself.

"It doesn't matter whether she knows it or not," Brian said, raising his voice. "There's one less married couple in the universe. That's a physical fact, even if nobody knows it. A fact is a fact, right? And every corner of the universe is affected by it."

"Well," the professor said, suddenly serious, "there may be one less married couple in the universe, that's true, but it has no physical significance for the Doctor's wife, nor for anyone else for that matter, not if no one knows about it."

"You mean," Brian asks, "if no one knows she's a widow, then she's not a widow?"

"Exactly,' the professor said. "Logically, yes, she's a widow, but it means nothing, it has no physical significance for her if no one on her spaceship knows about it."

"OK, OK," Brian said, 'but suppose before he left Herr Doctor buys a lottery ticket, and then on the rocket, before he dies, he finds out that he's won. He's the only one who knows about it. What you're saying is that the Doctor is rich now but the Frau Doctor isn't. She'll be rich later on." Brian had to giggle at the thought.

The professor frowned. "What I'm saying is that truths are truths and events are events. Lottery drawings are events that have to be communicated for them to mean anything," he said. "You're getting them confused, young fellow," the professor said with a paternal shake of his head.

Brian was stopped by that for a moment and had to look down to marshal his thoughts. Then, raising his head in triumph he cried, "OK, so what you're saying is that truths have no physical effects until they are communicated. And what I'm saying is that truths can have physical effects whether they are communicated or not. In my example, the physical effect is simultaneous."

"And just what are these physical effects?" the professor asked.

"Frau Doctor has become a rich widow," Brian shouted almost springing off the floor, "and the tax people are already figuring out what she owes."

The professor saw by now that he had been entertaining adolescent nonsense. The hour was up anyway so he waved to the class with a gesture of bemused futility and began to gather his notes.

Before long Brian was standing alone in the front of an empty hall, plunging his hands deep into bushy hair, student laughter still echoing in his ears. Actually the laughter didn't bother Brian that much. What really concerned him was the question of what old Einstein would have thought. Competitive though he was with his surrogate father, Einstein's opinion still mattered to the boy.

The hall was not entirely empty. The bright young woman from the front row had stayed behind. She came up to Brian and said, "Hi, there. You know that took a lot of nerve."

"He didn't get it," Brian said. "He didn't get anything I said."

"He's a physicist," she laughed. "Physicists can't take anything seriously unless it shows up somewhere on a meter."

Brian looked at her appreciatively. "I'm Brian," he said. "What's your name?"

"Penny," she said. Brian saw that she had a nice smile.

"Care for a beer?" he said.

"A beer!" she said. She laughed. "How old are you anyway?"

"We can go to Tony's," Brian said. "They know me there."

Penny hesitated. "Sure, why not," she said finally. "Everyone's talking about you, you know. The boy with the Einstein complex," she said pointing to his head.

They both laughed and set out for Tony's, Brian as unselfconscious as ever and this bright young lady piqued with curiosity. On the way Brian told her a joke he made up on the spot. There were these two physicists who had been working for years on a grand unified Theory of Everything, all laid out in a single equation on the blackboard. The day they worked out the last details they opened a bottle of champagne to celebrate.

"One of the physicists, lets call him A," Brian said, "when he went home after that, discovered his house had burned down and his wife had left him. He had a heart attack and wound up in the hospital. When B, the other physicist, came to visit him, he found A looking very worried. 'What's wrong?' B said. 'It's our Theory of Everything,' A said. 'I have this gut feeling we may have left something out.'"

That gave Brian and Penny another good laugh.

At Tony's Brian ordered a diet coke and a beer. When the drinks were delivered, Brian reached for the beer.

"Underage drinking," Penny said with her ready laugh. "You're going to get me in trouble." She was all of eighteen, itself not unprecocious for a Princeton junior.

Brian took a big gulp. He made a face and took another gulp. Then he wiped his mouth with his sleeve and leaned over towards his new friend.

"What to hear about my new law?" he said.

"Sure," she laughed, sipping coke. "Why not."

"OK," Brian said. "Here it is: *Nothing exists by itself.*"

"That's silly," she said. "It doesn't say anything."

"It says everything," Brian protested.

"*Nothing exists by itself,*" she repeated. "It just states the obvious."

"So what if it's obvious," he said. "It's important. Suppose the opposite were true."

"It's just silly," she said.

"It's anything but silly," he said. "The shortest distance between two points is a straight line. That's obvious too. Is it silly? Everybody's been quoting Euclid about it for two thousand years."

"But what's the point?" Penny said. "You can build on Euclid. What can anybody do with this silly law of yours?"

"My law is fundamental," Brian insisted. "Name something in the universe that doesn't depend on it."

Penny pushed her drink away. "You're cute," she said. The young lady made a move to get up. "You know I really shouldn't be here," she said. "I have exams tomorrow."

"You don't get it either," Brian said slumping back in his chair.

"OK," Penny said, settling back. "Explain it."

Brian took a paper napkin and wrote out his equation, R = M + O. He explained what each of the variables represented. The variable O stood for the Observer. M is the Material world, the raw stuff the observer looks at. And R is Cosmic Reality, the final combination of M and O taken together.

"Yeah," Brian said, "Einstein looked at the material world, at M, through the eyes of an observer, O, but with him, if there's no observer, no O, then there's no M, no world, and therefore no R, no Reality, no nothing. That's where he's wrong. His whole methodology is backwards. He's turned the world upside-down."

Penny laughed but the music was minor key. "Oh, really?" she said.

"Yeah," Brian said, "and for another thing, his observer isn't real. He's a cardboard character."

Brian emptied the beer bottle into his glass and took a big swig, wiping his mouth with his sleeve in that ritual way. Then he held up the bottle. "Look," he said, "you know what the world has in common with this bottle?"

Penny gave Brian a smirky smile and shook her head playfully. "I can't imagine," she said. "Tell me."

"They're both *things*," Brian said. "Right? And do you know what makes this bottle a *thing*, what makes the world a *thing?*"

Penny's smile faded. It's not that easy for a bright young junior to abide a freshmen bent on enlightening mankind, especially a motor-mouth who has yet to shave, even if he is cute.

"OK, I'll tell you," Brian said. "*We* do. We, the observer, we make them *things*. That's what my equation says, right? Sure, this bottle exists without us looking at it, but what is it? It's not a bottle, it's an organized flux of spinning particles or whatever. Without the observer it's not a bottle, not to this table, not to a fly on the wall, not to the moon. It's not a bottle to itself. And the world isn't a world either, it's just some swirling 'whatever' until observer O in my equation comes along. Even the spinning particles are our constructs, for God's sake," Brian said, voice rising.

Penny's expression became pure smirk as she glanced around at the neighboring tables. "Didn't Einstein say as much," she said in a calming tone. "We take in sense impressions and turn them into objects, isn't that what every physicist says?"

"Einstein's observers are stick figures," Brian said loud as ever, "and stick figures can only give you a matchstick world. It takes a real observer to make a real world with real things in it. Einstein's observer is a dreamed-up fiction he used for his thought experiments."

Others at a nearby table began looking their way and Penny frowned. "Brian," she said quietly, "you're getting light years away from physics, into biology or sociology, or who knows what. Maybe even religion." She let out a little laugh. "You should meet my boyfriend Ivan. You and he would get along famously." She summoned a nice smile and began to gather her things.

"Wait, listen," Brian said calming back down. "OK, sure, physics is different from biology and the rest, but you don't have physics without an observer, right? And you don't have an observer without biology and a lot of other stuff. Look," he said, "real observers just don't measure and calculate, they live and breathe and worry about tenure and have kids. How can you understand the world if you don't understand the observer that science depends on? Like, how did the flux, the M in my equation, produce O so that the M flux could observe itself? How did we get this O? Einstein never answered that question. He never even asked it."

Penny put her things down. "OK, Brian," she said with a laugh. "You have all the answers. Where did this observer, this O of yours come from?"

Brian looked at Penny, took a swig of beer and broke out into a grin. "You're the physicist," he said. "You tell me."

Penny rolled her eyes and looked around for her ready laugh. "OK," she said finally. "From the Big Bang, courtesy of natural selection. Where else?"

"You're saying that O came from M, then," Brian said. "From the raw stuff, the flux."

"Absolutely," Penny said. "Where else is this O of yours supposed to come from? "

"Where did the Big Bang come from?" Brian said.

"Who knows," Penny said rather more weakly, sensing a trap.

"Exactly," Brian said eager to spring it. "We don't know where flux M came from and we don't know where observer O came from either. If we can live with one unknown, what's wrong with two?"

"Come on Brian," Penny said. "Why bring in another singularity? One mystery is enough."

Brian was quick to answer. "If you can't explain how the raw M flux could produce its own observer, then you're stuck with a mystery like it or not. And so far no one has a clue. So if we can live with one mystery, we can live with two, right? Why not? Why not a Big Bang singularity to explain M, and a Silent Touch singularity to give us O. Did you ever see Michelangelo's painting where that old figure stretches out his finger to touch the young guy's finger? That young guy is observer O in my equation. He's getting his job assignment. He has to get up off his butt and give M, the flux, its finishing touches." Brian began to giggle at the thought.

"Brian, you're just a hopeless poet at heart," Penny said. "Not even a very good one maybe, but you're definitely cute," she added with a laugh.

Brian stopped, took a final slug of beer and looked over at Penny. "That's where Einstein lost it," he said. "What does a stick figure know about the sticky leaves?"

"*The sticky leaves,*" Penny repeated with a big laugh. "My boyfriend Ivan would definitely enjoy that. He's a liberal arts major and a Dostoevsky freak. He's crazy just like you."

Brian paid no attention but suddenly his eyes lit up. He grabbed the napkin he had just thrown down and began stabbing his finger at the equation. "I just realized something," he cried. "The R in my equation, the Cosmic Reality, it's not the *sum* of M and O. It's the *product*." Brian jumped up from his chair. "Yeah, that's it," he cried, knocking the beer bottle over. Penny had to keep it from rolling off the table.

"Take it easy, Brian," she said. "You almost broke your world."

"No, listen," Brian said flopping back down into his chair. "I really have it now," he said. He reached for the napkin. He crossed out the old equation and wrote a new one under it:

$$\cancel{R = M + O}$$
$$R = M * O$$

"That's really got it," he said, excitement rising again. "The O isn't something that's *added* to M. O *magnifies* M. Don't you get it?" he cried. "R is their *product*, the *product* of M and O. That's what gives us our incredible world with its sticky leaves and all."

"Brian, quiet down," Penny said reaching out to calm him.

"Listen," Brian cried shaking her off, "what happens if you took O out of R, if there's no observer left in the world. Reality just shrivels up, right? All you'd have is the spinning particles, the raw M. You can assemble all the cans of paint and brushes and canvases you want but they'll never make a picture. That takes an artist, right? That's the O in my equation. A living artist, not a stick figure."

"Oh, Brian," Penny said gathering her things, "you don't belong in physics. They'll eat you alive."

"They shoved Einstein aside too," Brian threw back at her. "Until he published his papers and knocked the world for a loop."

"Don't hold your breath," Penny said getting to her feet. But as she turned to leave she reached down and took the napkin and tucked it into her purse. "Just in case I'm wrong," she said with her ready laugh.

Brian did not watch her go. His hands were furrowed deep into Einstein hair as if he was trying to grab hold of his brain (Brian's brain), maybe to cool it down.

Then suddenly his mind raced off into something he knew he had to do.

He had to get in touch with Einstein. He had to know what the master thought of his ideas. Brian got his bike and rode over to Einstein's old place on Mercer Street. He stopped in front of the small, white, two-story frame house, lived in now by strangers, and imagined going up to the door and Einstein letting him in. They would exchange a few words and then Einstein would take him up to his tiny office on the second floor in the back and they would sit and talk. He would ask Einstein why, if he built his entire system on the observer and the fact that you can't say anything about the world except what the observer observes, why did Einstein end up turning the observer into a bloodless measuring device? No doubt about it, Einstein would have something to say. And Brian would show him where he was wrong. A bloodless observer is just a piece of equipment and what does equipment have to do with the really real?

Brian moved on past the house and biked down

the tree-lined street towards the Institute where Einstein had his office, along with the other mental giants working there. There were woods by the Institute with paths Einstein used to like to walk. Brian turned his bike down one of these paths and then, a ways into the woods, he stopped. It had rained earlier and the fall-colored leaves were dripping as a breeze stirred the trees. The late afternoon sun had come back out, its soft light creeping through the branches.

Brian got off his bike and sat on a rock. The rock was wet and he could feel the dampness run through his trousers. He got up and felt the seat of his pants. It struck him that he knew the rock was damp because his seat was damp and his seat was damp because he felt the dampness on his skin. As if the dampness were there only because he felt it. He remembered reading what Plato had said about a tree falling in the forest. If no one was there to hear it, Plato asked, would it make a sound? Brian looked at the wet foliage everywhere around him. Would anything be wet and damp without his being there to see it and feel it? He stooped over and ran his hands through a pile of leaves. The fallen leaves were wet and slimy and cool to his hand. Were the leaves slimy and cool by themselves, without him? He looked up at the trees all around him, wet leaves glistening like jewels in the setting light as a gentle movement of air stirred the branches. He heard in the distance a car door slam back at the Institute. He could hear distant voices. This had been Einstein's little world. He must have come here on afternoons like this to get away and must have felt the same autumn cool, smelled the same dampness rising from the earth, watched the peek-a-boo of sunlight in the leaves. Did he have the same reflections? Brian wondered. Now it was Brian's world, for as long as he stood there. And when he left, when no one was there, what would happen to the woods? What would be left? Something, but not wet, fall-colored trees and the smells of fallen leaves beginning to rot. No, just a mess of spinning, nameless "whatever." He imagined Einstein stopping here, looking around, he too giving the woods its forms, its hues, shadows, the glitter of sunlight, the hardness of the macadam underfoot where he stood, the stillness, the brush of fresh cool breeze against the face. None of it was here without a beating heart to see, feel, smell, listen, even taste the woods. The woods were here because he, Brian, was here, and Einstein before him, and anyone else coming here and taking in the spinning "whatever" and giving back the world. No piece of equipment could begin to do that. Why didn't Einstein get it?

Brian walked his bike along the path. He stopped before a puddle where a sparrow had been dipping its beak. It flew away as he approached, into a tree. He reflected that the sparrow had no idea of the puddle, it was just a place to drink, it didn't know water was water, only something that it must have, or that a tree was a tree, only a place to flee to. Only he, Brian, the privileged observer in his flesh and blood knew these things. Everything, the soft, the hard, the slimy, the wet, the cold, they were only there because he was there. Without him, the woods were just moving particles that spun around and around. Even the particles were constructions, courtesy of someone's theory. Who heard the noise in the Big Bang? Face it, there was no bang. Who saw that first primeval flash of light? Without a retina, how can you speak of light? Without a flesh and blood observer, the world utters no sound, casts no shadows, never gets wet or dry, never turns hard or soft, hot or cold. Just raw spinning "whatever" organizing itself in some way so that some observer could come along into the world someday, into these woods, and color it all in and say, you're a tree, you're a puddle, a rock, the breeze, the setting sun, the galaxy Andromeda, the universe. Einstein said there's no place for subjectivity in physics. No need for a flesh and blood observer. But why? What is the objective world without a flesh and blood subject? Why didn't Einstein ask how the nameless flux, this M, could produce flesh and blood so that flesh and blood, the observer, the O could produce this world, our reality, this incredible R with all its magnificence, giving it and all the things that are in it, their names, their colors, their textures?

A fresh breeze came up and stirred the branches, showering Brian with cool, dripping rain. He didn't move. He stood there leaning on his bike, looking around, the stand of white birches in the woods just ahead, bushy foliage everywhere losing color, patches of slippery moss along the path, green as old wine bottles. Brian stayed there without moving, dumbstruck, not at the stillness of a late afternoon woods dripping with an autumn rain and the flicker of liquid sunlight. Brian closed his eyes. It was something else entirely. "None of this is there without me," he said, the words sounding only in his racing mind. "It's all for me," he said. "It's all for me." Brian felt giddy, as if he were floating, his feet no longer touching the damp macadam path.

But then, as was his way, in the very next moment Brian saw something else. He spotted a squirrel poised by a tree watching him, ready to scamper off if he moved. Brian watched him back.

"Yeah," Brian thought, "this little guy has his world too. This is his territory and I'm messing it up for him right now. My world and the squirrel's world are worlds apart, but it didn't matter. Here we are connecting, trading stares. He doesn't know he's a squirrel to me, and I don't know what I am to him, but we're here for each other, we're here for each other."

Then, in that wet afternoon instant, everything that had been happening to this boy Brian since coming to Princeton slipped into place. Yes, it was true, *nothing exists by itself*, but there was a corollary that went even deeper, and this fourteen-year-old Einstein kid finally knew what it was.

The truth is, of course, the kid Brian had a lot more to learn about a great many things, not the least of which was himself. He might just possibly be as smart as Einstein (not likely of course) but, for one thing, he was not even one hundredth as humble. True, humility is not always easy to find in science, and in that respect Einstein seemed to be rather unusual, so it would make an interesting story how Brian might have learned it, if ever he did. The present account only takes us to the point where Brian was informed — along with his mother — that he would not be allowed to declare for physics, not now or ever, not at Princeton. It was a judgment arrived at by the entire physics faculty to a man (no women then on the physics faculty), no doubt instigated by Zelnitsky. The boy might be rather gifted, it was half-acknowledged, and might do well in some other field, but certainly not in physics. Metaphysics perhaps.

The incident that brought this denouement about, Zelnitsky's last straw, deserves to be told. It transpired that the famous Italian physicist, Piero Pieri, reputed Noble Prize shortlister, was giving a lecture at Princeton. Zelnitsky had gone to great lengths to get this prize speaker and was restricting attendance to Princeton faculty and just the physics grad students and upper-class undergrads. And of course the faulty and postdocs at the Institute for Advanced Studies nearby. It was to be a gala affair, with a reception following. Piero Pieri was reporting on his collaboration with Stephen Hawking and other cosmologists on one of the hottest topics of the day. The posters on the bulletin boards in the physics department put it plainly enough: "Is Time Like an Arrow Or Can We Travel to the Past?"

It was a fluke that Brian was able to attend. On the day of the lecture, he bumped into Penny by chance and asked her if she were going. Penny explained it was her birthday and her boyfriend Ivan wanted to celebrate so that was that.

140

"And what are you going to do with your ticket?" Brian asked.

"You'd like to have it, I suppose," Penny said, going into her purse. "But you have to promise me you'll behave," she said. "Zelnitsky will kill me if you don't." Brian didn't promise anything of the sort, of course. "Just don't let him know where you got it, oh, please," Penny said handing it over. Brian said thanks, but wishing her a happy birthday, sadly, was still beyond the reach of a boy still pretty much stuck in his own thoughts.

The hall that evening was quite full. Zelnitsky was seated in the front row center, surrounded by most of the physics faculty along with faculty from the Institute. Postdocs, grad students and upper-class types were everywhere else. Brian got there early and took a seat way off to the side a few rows behind Zelnitsky, more or less out of his line of sight.

Before long the hall was alive with expectation.

Piero Pieri began to talk about time warps and the prospects of reversing time and actually revisiting the past. Prospects for that he said were not unthinkable, as he was about to demonstrate. There were lots of equations on the board and probably no one in the audience followed entirely, not even Zelnitsky, and certainly not Brian. But equations are equations, part intimidation, part seduction, even when true. Capturing cosmic eons in an equation, no matter how arcane, has its lures.

Near the end of the lecture, Piero Pieri smiled out at the gathering and said he wanted say a few final words now, not about the past but about the present. About our illusions regarding this particular aspect of time. He said that all of us, even cosmologists, live personal lives operating under an absolutely naive and theoretically incorrect notion of the present.

"Our idea of what we call 'the present world' is simply false," he said. "In what sense is the world in fact ever present to us?"

To illustrate this, he said, "Let us assume that there are two objects in the universe, X and Y, and ask the question: in what sense can we say that any X is present to any Y, that X and Y co-exist in each other's present timeframe, like two actors appearing on the stage at the same moment? Of course," Piero Pieri went on, "as Einstein pointed out, we know that true simultaneity of any two events in the universe is theoretically impossible. So, if X is a galaxy millions of light years away, and Y is an observer on the earth looking at its starlight, X is only present to Y in an historical sense. We know in fact that it is quite possible X no longer exists and is no longer emitting light. So we can never say that X is present to Y. Only its past is present."

"Now," Piero Pieri went on, "let us move X closer and assume that X is the sun, 93 millions miles away from Y, our observer on the earth. According to Newton's action-at-a-distance, if the sun were to suddenly cease to exist, the loss of its gravitational tug on the earth would be felt virtually at once and Y would know it right away. But we now know it would take a full eight minutes before Y would feel the sun's demise. So when Y looks up at the sun, he could be seeing something that ceased to exist as many as eight minutes ago. He could continue to bask in the sun's rays for those eight minutes but what he is enjoying is the sun's past, not its present. And that's always the case.

"Now let's move X closer still, say, to someone standing one meter away from observer Y. Like everything else, Y is aware of X on the basis of signals X gives off. The fastest signal Y can receive from X is light. So Y sees X and knows that X is present on the basis of light travel. But here again, strictly speaking, what Y knows about X is only something true of X in the past. An extremely recent past to be sure, for light travels the distance of one meter in 3.3 billionths of a second. 3.3 billionths of a second is not much elapse of time, indeed, but the past is the past.

"I think the point is clear enough," Piero Pieri said. "No matter how we define X, whether as a distant galaxy, as the sun, or the person standing next to Y, Y's experience of X is always an experience of X's past. The only difference in these examples is the interval that separates X from Y. In the case of the most distant galaxy, the interval can be 13.37 billion light years, in the case of the bystander, 3 billionths of a second. That is not much time, agreed, and in everyday life we can ignore it. But in physics, the situation can be very different. Consider this: in the interval of 10 to the minus 10 seconds after the Big Bang singularity, i.e., in one billionth of a second after everything got started, there were already formed all the quarks, protons and neutrons that are needed to create hydrogen, helium, lithium, deuterium, in short, virtually all the matter that makes up our universe today. All this in the interval of one billionth of a second. So we see that in the interval it takes Y to blink as Y looks at X right next to him, a lot can have already happened.

"So what does this really mean," Piero Pieri asked. "It means that the only thing truly present to Y is Y itself, whatever Y is. We can think of Y as our consciousness, our self-awareness, and say that our self-possession alone encompasses the entire meaning of 'present time', but even that may be naive. The X and Y problem is still with us. For what is consciousness, after all, but a configuration of brain synapses, networks of neurons interacting. And inside these interactions are billions of X's and Y's, cells that must signal other cells through some wall of time. It's the problem of galaxies in another key," he said. "And of what do these neurons consist but the very particles that were formed in that billionth of a second interval after the Big Bang. All these atomic particles are also just so many interacting X's and Y's therefore, all separated by this wall of elapsed time. So in the end, we are forced to conclude that the only thing that is truly present to itself is the indivisible particle—if there even is such a thing—With each such particle isolated from every other particle by some interval of time imposed by the speed of light.

"The universe is a terribly lonely place therefore," Piero Pieri said in his wrap up. "And from a cosmologist's perspective, as the universe keeps expanding, it can only get lonelier. The world we enjoy is already past tense. And who knows," he concluded, "perhaps our fascination with travel to the past is driven by secret dread of a present tense that is already synonymous with cosmic loneliness."

At this Piero Pieri sat down to an abundance of applause and appreciative nods. Zelnitsky glanced around at those about him, proud as a peacock.

The applause and smiles and nods had hardly died down before Brian's voice could be heard addressing the speaker. "What if X and Y are one and the same?" he cried. He had to shout it several times before the hall was quiet enough to gain the speaker's attention.

"One and the same?" Piero Pieri repeated, getting back on his feet. "What is this?" he said, moving to the edge of the platform.

In a move as near to simultaneity as Einstein's theory would permit, Zelnitsky was also up on his feet.

Brian came forward and stood immediately before the speaker's platform. "What if X and Y are the same thing?" he shouted to be heard. "What if they're the same person?"

Piero Pieri peered down at the strange boy confronting him. "I don't understand this question," he said. He looked over at Zelnitsky, then back at the boy's head of hair.

"OK," Brian shouted. "What if Y bi-locates? What about bi-location?"

Piero Pieri looked around. "What is this bi-location?" he said.

Brian drew himself up. "You know, the padre from your country who bi-locates. Padre Pion or something."

"Pion? Pion?" Piero Pieri repeated puzzled, looking over to Zelnitsky for help.

"Yeah, Brian" shouted. "He was a monk. I read about him. They just made him a saint or something. Padre Pion."

There was laughter in the audience at this. Some crypto-Catholic in the audience, no longer able contain himself, shouted out "*Padre Pio, Padre Pio.*"

"Right," Brian said, "Padre Pio. Lots of people saw him in two places at once. There's plenty of data. X and Y in two different places at the exact same time."

"Is this serious?" Piero Pieri said looking accusingly at Zelnitsky. Zelnitsky, beside himself, started towards Brian.

"No, listen," Brian shouted, dancing away. "Suppose when he bi-locates the padre is wearing a watch. The two padres both have the same time then, right? The minute hands on both watches are moving simultaneously. It's the same watch, right? So there's no time elapse, no past, no wall of time between them. So if they're the same thing, X and Y can be present to each other, right? One hundred percent, no matter how far apart. All you have to do is bi-locate." Brian began to giggle.

Zelnitsky motioned to two of the younger instructors to lead Brian away. Which is what they did and how Brian's budding career as a budding physicist ended on the spot. But as they led him away, the boy managed to get off some good parting salvos about simultaneity and loneliness and how *nothing exists by itself,* all to the amusement of those who could hear him, save of course our long-suffering Chair.

Brian ran into Penny and her boyfriend Ivan not long after Brian's fate had become general knowledge.

"Brian," she said, "I heard. I'm so sorry."

Brian said, "It's OK. It's bothered my mother more than me."

Penny introduced Ivan and said she had told her boyfriend some of his crazy ideas. She said he liked the bit about "sticky leaves."

"Yeah, man," Ivan said, "that's my kind of talk." He patted his girl friend on the head. "I keep telling her there's more truth in a butterfly than in $E=mc^2$."

Brian just looked at him and Penny made a face. "And I told Ivan about your law," she went on, laughing again. She went into her purse and took out the napkin with Brian's equation on it. She held it up.

Nothing exists by itself.

"That's true religion man," Ivan said. "What you say goes right to the top."

When Brian looked at him blankly, Ivan added, "The *Trinity*, man, the *Trinity*."

Brian brightened. "I've even made it better," he said.

"Awesome, brother, awesome," Ivan said.

Penny studied Brian for a moment. "I heard about the Padre Pio bit the other night," she said. "Were you thinking of your law?"

"Not really," Brian said. "Maybe. Bi-location can be predicted by my law, you know."

Penny smiled and shook her head. "You really don't belong in physics," she said.

"Why not?" Brian said. "Physics deals with whatever's the case, right? Wherever it takes you."

Penny kept studying Brian. "Brian," she said, "physics will never stomach this subjectivity kick of yours. There's enough uncertainty in physics as it is. No two people ever see the same event the same way. You can't do science that way, you know that. In physics you try *not* to interact with the world. The idea is you watch it and measure it. You stand off at a distance and try to figure out what makes it tick."

Brian shook his head. "What can you know about anything if you don't relate to it," he said. Brian took the napkin out of Penny's hand and, leaning against a wall, wrote a second phrase beneath his original handwriting.

"Here," he said passing it back, "I added a new axiom. The two together sum up my law."

> *Nothing exists by itself*
> *Nothing exists for itself*

"Oh, Brian," Penny said, "this isn't physics."

"Maybe," Brian said, "but it takes more than a slide rule to know what's what. I told you that before," he said looking at Penny like she was the hopeless one, "but you still don't get it. Look, the O in my equation is the set of all beating heart observers. And they interact with the raw ingredients of the Big Bang, the M, and that interaction gives us R, our marvelous reality, the world as we know it."

Then Brian's face lit up. He took the napkin from Penny and added an exponent to the O in the equation, crossing out the earlier one.

$$\sout{R = M * O}$$
$$R = M * O^2$$

"The observers interact with each other, too," he said, handing it back to her, thinking of the squirrel. "That pretty much says it all," he said. "The world is the product of the raw 'whatever' of the Big Bang multiplied by the square of beating heart observers."

Brian took it from her again and re-wrote the equation to parallel Einstein's $E=mc^2$.

$$R=mo^2$$

"*Nothing exists by itself, nothing exists for itself,*" he said with off-hand solemnity, as if it should be obvious to everyone. "A bi-locating monk would get it," he added giving it back to Penny with the barest trace of a smile. Then the smile widened at the thought of the original fantasy that had started him off — the bi-locating master, *Ein*-stein, *Zwei*-stein.

"Far out, man, I like it," Ivan said slapping Brian on the back. $R=mo^2$ has got Einstein beat by beaucoup light years." Nudging his girlfriend he said, "He's making space for the butterflies and sticky leaves."

Penny shook her head forlornly. "Brian, you're totally impractical," she said. "What can you do with this? The heart can't split atoms, can't launch a space probe to Mars, can't even earn a living for that matter."

"It can say 'this is good,' 'all is well,' and 'go to hell,'" Brian said, looking at her with a funny smile.

"Cool, man, cool," Ivan said trying to give Brian a high five, but Brian didn't want to play.

"I'll tell you what you can do with it," Brian said still pondering Penny's question. "Nobody's going to give up his life, actually die for an equation, not even E=mc² , right? But somebody might, you know, for a friend. What does physics really know if it doesn't know that?"

With a face of sad frustration Penny looked at the napkin. *Nothing exists for itself.* She spoke each of the words deliberately, like they were in a foreign tongue. Then she looked over at the boy with the Einstein mop standing before her, not even her height. "So tell me, Brian," she said, "and who do you exist for?"

The boy Brian for once had no answer, but it's not so strange, after all. He was just a brainy kid with a complex. All he wanted to do was to prove the father he loved was wrong. But that, like everything else we know of this world, is only half the story.

My reader, if you will indulge the narrator for one more moment, let me share this fantasy of how the story ends, not in the near term, mind you, but way down the cosmic pike, when the Cosmic Artist has laid down his brush and all the spinning flux set in motion 14 billion years ago, or whenever it was, has finally come to rest. It's a picture of amazing felicity.

I see Brian and Einstein in a luminous place, both now fully enlightened, both fully aware now that *you can truly know and understand only what you truly love.* They are walking arm in arm and laughing, and by some merry dispensation of Providence, both still needing a haircut.

Physicist's Postscript

Here is a telling remark by the justly famous Noble prizewinner, Erwin Schroedinger, a physicist I believe Brian would have loved to take a beer with. I just can see Brian, at some point, suggesting they raise a glass to good old human subjectivity.

"I cannot believe that the deep philosophical enquiry into the relation between subject and object and into the true meaning of the distinction between them depends upon the quantitative results of physical and chemical measurements with weighing scales, spectroscopes, microscopes, telescopes, with Geiger-Mueller counters, Wilson chambers, photographic plates, arrangements for measuring the radioactive decay, and whatnot. It is not easy for me to say why I do not believe it. I feel a certain incongruity between the applied means and the problem to be solved."

—from his *Science and Humanism,*
quoted in Niels Bohr, *A Centenary Volume,* p. 131.